Forbidden Bonds

Reforming the Paranormal Council

Book One

Forbidden Bonds

Reforming the Paranormal Council

Book One

Sheri Eleese

First Edition September 2020
Third Printing 2022
ISBN 978-1-7773217-2-7

Cover Design: SelfPubBookCovers.com/Joetherasakdhi

Table of Contents

Acknowledgements

To start off with, I'd like to send a big thanks to my brother, Bruce. This book wouldn't have been written if he hadn't reminded me that once upon a time, I had a dream. A dream that had been buried and forgotten, living life and doing adult things. Because of your encouragement, I'm now having the greatest time living my best life. Because you told me I deserve it. So thanks. I owe you one, Bruce.

A big thanks also goes to my Mom, Lynn, who had the pleasure of reading the first draft and listening to me ramble on and on about the storyline. You helped me find the initial plot holes and asked some key questions that helped with the development of the next drafts. Your patience, excitement, and loving support means the world to me. Thanks for being the best Mom ever.

To my fantastic beta readers Ashley and Angela. My thanks for your time and efforts. You helped in ways you don't even know and your unconditional support made this journey so much more exciting and fun.

Ashley, thank you for your suggestions that improved the writing as a whole and for steering me in the right direction when I went astray. The added personal comments were a hoot and made me laugh. So. Hard.

Angela, thank you for pointing out those pesky little timing issues and finding numerous errors that really needed to be fixed. Your willingness to help me choose when I'm stuck between A, B, and C, is also greatly appreciated.

Last, but not least, a super big thanks to my son, James, who helped with the copy editing after everyone else had done their part, finding the minutest mistakes. James, your help and support, and listening to your mom's endless story explanations, was amazing. Especially since you really don't like anything about the genre, theme, or the kissing. I couldn't have done it without you buddy. Love you.

Any mistakes left behind are all on me, as I obviously messed, once again, with the final draft. True story.

I'd also like to send a big thanks to all my friends and family who showed their love and support with texts, phone calls, FB posts, and messages. Your support means the world to me. Love you guys.

And to Jen, I found a way to sneak it in here. Happy reading

Prologue

"Do we have an accord?" Graceful hands gripped the receiver firmly, French tipped nails turning white from the pressure. "Yes, it shouldn't be a problem. I'll have the youngest boy at the altar next month."

Nails began clicking on the desk with irritation as the voice from the receiver began speaking faster. "Do not worry yourself. His older brother will not be a problem. I can control him."

More agitated words.

"Are you questioning me? Perhaps you have forgotten who's in charge."

The disembodied voice lowered, the next question asked hesitantly.

"Correct. Once the boy has produced an offspring, we will begin. Luckily, we know the girl can breed."

Agitated words started up again.

Impatient with the continued excuses, she cut him off. "Make no mistake, that was a failure on your part and will cause us much delay. Do not fail me again." She paused as the voice continued. "The boy? Do what you will with him after. All we need is the child."

Sheri Eleese

Chapter One

Lysander Galway stepped through the door of Darkness and stopped, looking for his best friend, Tommy, who had called earlier that day demanding his presence as wingman for a new guy he was pursuing. Tommy had the worst luck finding men, so Lysander fully expected the night to turn into a disaster. However, when your best friend asks for a favor, you show up.

His searching eyes caught and held on the most beautiful man he'd ever seen. He froze in place as he thoroughly cataloged all the gorgeous parts of tall, dark, and handsome, starting with the long, ebony hair that reached down to his waist. He was dressed all in black, his silk shirt showing off his broad shoulders to perfection. Lysander ran his eyes down long, muscular legs that ended in black leather boots. Sighing to himself, he rested his gaze on the aristocratic face, noting the dark eyes, long, patrician nose, and full, decadent lips. The object of his fascination was in conversation with another man, giving off the vibe that he was the man in charge, the master of his universe. Lysander narrowed his eyes as he studied the man, wondering if it was confidence or arrogance. One was super sexy, the other, not so much. Shrugging, Lysander decided it didn't matter. It wasn't as if he was going to marry the guy. He started in the man's direction, looking forward to having a taste.

Unfortunately, duty by the name of Tommy called. Or rather, shouted at him from across the room.

"Lysander, over here." Tommy waved at him, then fell against the edge of the bar. He pushed himself back, then motioned him over, swaying in his chair.

Lysander groaned. Awesome. His role had switched from wingman to babysitter even faster than he'd expected.

"Hey, Tommy. How's it going, bud?"

"Not good. Not good at all." Shaking his head, Tommy downed half his glass in a single swallow. "I gave it my best shot, but he turned me down flat. Says he's looking for someone with boobs, Ell. And I don't have any." He lifted his shirt, smacking his well-defined chest with one hand. "See, none at all. I'm just a guy with no boobs." Tommy raised his glass, then took a drink, giggling into his glass and chanting what sounded like no boobs, no boobs on me.

Lysander's eyes widened, unable to believe what he was hearing. This was so much worse than he'd thought. How could Tommy be this drunk already? It was barely past nine.

"I'm sorry to hear that, Tommy." Lysander put his hand on his friend's shoulder. "But here's a thought. Since this place is obviously a bust tonight, why don't we get out of here and grab some takeout. We can eat and watch a movie at my place."

Half-closed eyes looked at him as Tommy mulled that over, before eventually nodding. Smacking his lips, he said, "Sure. That sounds good. But no Netflix and chill." He snickered. "I love you, man, but only like a brother, so there won't be any of that." Tommy burped, then peered into his glass, and started snickering again. The Goddess only knew at what.

Lysander sighed as he stared at his ridiculous friend. He was going to mock him about this night for a very, very long time. Turning to the bar, Lysander gestured to the bartender, signaling to close out Tommy's tab. As the bartender brought it over, Tommy set his glass on the bar top, somehow unbalancing himself so he fell into Lysander. Seeing his friend in such a state sent his protective instincts into overdrive. And he knew just who to blame for his friend's condition.

When the bartender handed him the slip of paper, Lysander glared at him. "What the hell kind of place are you running here? I was told you took your patron's safety seriously in this place."

The bartender frowned. "We do. What's the problem?"

"You."

"Me? What did I do?"

"Look at him." Lysander pointed at Tommy. "He's a drunken mess. You have a responsibility to your patrons to cut them off long before they get like this?"

He wasn't expecting the bartender's laughter. "Look, pal. I had no idea your buddy was such a light-weight. He should come with a warning."

"I don't understand."

"I only served him three drinks. Maybe you should get him out of here." He slapped the tab down on the counter before moving to attend to a customer at the other end.

Lysander grabbed the paper. Sure enough, there were only three drinks on it. "For crying out loud, Tommy. I'm so embarrassed for you." He placed enough money on the bar top to cover the tab, then added a large tip as an apology. Wrapping his hand around Tommy's arm, he hauled his now loudly singing friend from his seat. "Time to go, Britney."

"I love you man."

"I know, buddy. I love you too. Let's get you out of here."

Turning to go, he bumped into the man he'd been eyeing up earlier. Whoa. He was even more amazing up close. Lysander leaned into the man, helplessly drawn to him.

"Can I invite you gentlemen to my private table?" Such a warm, rich, decadent voice; like smooth caramel drizzled over chocolate. Lysander leaned in closer, completely mesmerized.

A large hand rested on his shoulder as the man pointed to a reserved section on the other side of the bar. "It's just over there."

Lysander was about to say yes, when he realized Tommy was hanging heavier in his hold, almost enough to slip free. "Sorry, I can't."

"Are you sure?"

"Yes. I need to get my friend home. But thanks. Maybe next time."

"Perhaps I can change your mind."

"No. I need to go."

The man leaned closer, getting right into Lysander's face, and looking intently into his eyes. The hand on his shoulder tightened. "I insist. Please. Come with me."

Lysander started to say no again then got lost in his gaze, the words dying on his tongue. He felt a small tickle in his brain and found himself wanting to agree with anything the man said.

"Ell, I don't feel so good." Tommy shifted, bumping him and breaking his connection with the man.

Shaking the fog from his head, Lysander glared at tall, dark, and handsome, annoyed for some inexplicable reason.

"I said no. We're leaving." He looked pointedly at the man's hand, still resting on his shoulder, then shrugged it off. "Please excuse us."

Lysander dragged Tommy past the man. As they neared the exit, he looked over his shoulder and saw the man staring after him with what looked like a thoughtful expression on his face.

Turning away, Lysander could feel his eyes on him as he half-carried Tommy out the door to the sidewalk.

Once they were outside and free from the man's near-overwhelming presence, Lysander sighed. Mostly in disappointment that the man had proven to be an arrogant ass in not taking no for an answer. But also in regret at not getting a chance to taste him.

Shaking it off, he began the long walk home, dragging his inebriated and loudly singing best friend with him. Tommy was going to owe him big for this night.

"If I may say, that didn't go very well."

"Shut up, Max."

Max laughed. "I've never seen you get shot down quite like that before. Or so quickly."

"Max, that was my Bloodmate, my fated soulmate. And he just walked out on me."

"Oh." Max said, drawing the word out. "Damn."

Damn indeed.

* * *

The next day at the park…

Lysander tore the sketch off his pad, handing it to the excited lady who squealed when she saw his caricature of her. He tucked the money she gave him into his gratifyingly full satchel. It was looking like he'd have a nice amount to donate to this week's chosen charity. He'd found people placed greater value on something they'd paid for than if he gave it to them for free, so he'd started charging a modest fee for his work. But since he didn't need the money, he gave what he earned to help those less fortunate. His payment came in the form of having his work appreciated and treasured.

Motioning to the two kids who were next in line to come forward, he spared a moment to wonder how Tommy was feeling today. He'd barely gotten him home last night before he passed out. Lysander chuckled to himself, still amazed that Tommy had been plastered on such a small amount of alcohol.

Realizing the kids were waiting for him, Lysander smiled at the young boy and girl standing in front of him. "Hey guys, enjoying the sun today?"

"Yes, mister. Can we be in the picture together? It's for our mom's birthday."

"Of course. Did you guys want a lifelike one or something more like a cartoon?"

The boy and girl looked at each other, then started whispering. A moment later they started digging in their pockets, pulling out spare change and counting it carefully.

Lysander realized they probably wanted one of each. He did a rough count of the money they were pooling, then interrupted them, motioning them closer with his fingers.

"Hey guys, come here. I want to tell you a secret." When they moved in, he whispered, "I don't want everyone else to hear but I have a special rate for Mothers today. Especially if it's their birthday. You can get two pictures for one dollar. So maybe you could get one of each kind. Did you think that would make her happy?"

The frantic nods made his smile spread across his face. "Excellent. Why don't you guys sit on that bench there and we'll get started."

Humming to himself, Lysander began sketching. While he worked, memories of his encounter with the hottie last night crept into his thoughts, just like they'd been doing all day. He kept pushing them out, but that damn man kept sneaking back in. It was starting to piss him off.

Finished with his sketch, he ripped the page out of his book and handed it to the young girl, getting a brilliant smile in return. He grinned back at her, thinking it was the best payment he'd received all day. The boy started bouncing in his seat, obviously impatient for his picture. Lysander winked at him. "Hang tight, buddy. Just a few more minutes, then I'll be done with yours." He got to work, quickly sketching the caricature. Finished, he handed it over, chuckling over the happy noises he got in return.

The young girl giggled, pointing. "Look how big our heads are."

"Whoa, mister. This is awesome. Mom's going to love it." The boy dug in his pocket, pulling out coins. He slowly counted out the correct change, then proudly handed it over. "Thank you. This will be the best gift ever. C'mon, Janey, I want to go show dad." He grabbed her hand and started dragging her away. "Thanks again, mister."

Lysander smiled and waved, then motioned the next person forward. Beginning his drawing of the man sitting in front of him, he noticed a car driving slowly down the street on his side of the park. Speaking of strange. He frowned, watching from the corner of his eye as it drove past him. This was about the fourth time he'd seen that same car this morning. Not a car guy, the only reason it had caught his attention was that it wasn't every day a fancy black luxury car with a driver drove around his neighborhood.

As it went past, Lysander lifted his head and focused on the heavily tinted windows. No matter how hard he tried, he couldn't see who was riding in the back of the car. But what really bothered him was the feeling of being watched. Which was ridiculous. Who would want to follow him around? Shaking his head at his overactive imagination, he got back to his sketch.

* * *

Lysander walked home from the park, whistling a jaunty tune. It was a bright sunny afternoon, the birds were singing, bees were buzzing, and his soul felt recharged. After a week of dealing with ongoing family drama, he'd needed a day like today. He'd met some amazing people and made a lot of money for charity. His pencil had seemed to fly across the paper. So much so, that it had been almost magical. Which was ironic, since lack of magic was the root of most of his troubles with his family.

"Hey young man. Can you spare some change?"

Lysander quickly pivoted, going to the man sitting in the alcove of a boarded up store. Crouching down, he fought not to react to the smell wafting off the man. "Good afternoon, Claude. No work for you today?"

Grinning at him, gaps showing from his missing teeth, Claude shook his head. "Not today. They take the young ones. Not an old fool like me."

"Have you had anything to eat?" He got a quick head shake. Okay then, sometimes charity started right in your own backyard. Lysander stood up and reached in his front pocket, pulling out a handful of crumpled bills. "Make sure you buy yourself something to eat with this. I want you to have a full stomach tonight?'

Claude nodded, quickly snatching the bills from his hand, then jumped up and hobbled down the street as quickly as his old limbs would carry him, turning into the diner near the corner.

Lysander continued down the sidewalk, impatient to get home. Approaching the final corner before his apartment, he saw young Sally Meyer with tears streaming down her face as she stared up a tree. Hurrying over, he crouched beside her, looking through the leaves to see where she was pointing. "Ahh, I see poor Sebastien has got himself into a pickle again."

Sally giggled through her tears, blowing mucus bubbles from her nose. "It's a tree, not a pickle, Mr. Lizzy. I keep telling you that."

Lysander laughed and stood, ruffling her hair. "True enough. Let's see if I can get him to come down from there." Moving under the tree, Lysander held out his hands, talking softly to the cat. "Sebastien, come here pretty kitty," he crooned to the frightened cat. Sending out encouraging vibes, Lysander reached as high as he could, hoping the cat would come to him. Sometimes he got lucky. That wasn't the case today.

"Really, Sebastien? You couldn't give me a break?" Cat eyes stared back at him unblinkingly. Lysander looked down, grimacing at his sandals, which were not the best footwear for climbing trees. Unfortunately, they were going to have to do.

He set his satchel at the base of the trunk, before shimmying up to the lowest branches. He maneuvered his feet onto the thicker section by the trunk, then pulled himself up to the next level, before sitting sideways, bracing himself on the trunk. Throwing his leg over to straddle the branch, he carefully inched toward the cat, crooning encouragement the entire time. Sebastien watched him, purring, as he patiently waited for his ride to arrive. Lysander rolled his eyes. Cats. Once he was close enough, he plucked him from the branch. Holding Sebastien to his chest, Lysander retreated down the tree, following the same path he took going up, the descent much more difficult with a purring cat in his arms. It was totally worth it, though, to stop a young girl's tears.

Safely on the ground, he handed a grateful Sally her trouble-making cat. "Thank you, Mr. Lizzy. I love you so much for saving my cat." She hugged him hard, as only a child could, squishing the cat between them. Sebastien gave an unhappy meow.

Lysander sighed ruefully at the tears and snot now decorating the front of his shirt. "I'm always happy to see you, Sally, but I think it's time to take Sebastien home now. He's had enough excitement for today."

"I will. Thank you again. C'mon, Sebastien. Let's go see if mom has any snacks for us."

"Goodbye, Sally. You two have a wonderful afternoon." Lysander turned to finish walking the remaining distance to his apartment, then stopped, frowning when he saw a black car going around the corner. Was that the same car he'd been seeing all day? No. It couldn't be. It must be a coincidence. Picking up his pace all the same, he tried to shake off the chill he suddenly felt, glad his building was only a short distance away.

* * *

The next morning…

Yawning, Lysander made sure the apartment security door closed properly behind him, his mouth already salivating thinking about his morning latte from the corner coffee shop. "Oh. Good morning, Miss Petrie," he greeted one of the tenants, rushing forward to grab her grocery bags before they could slip from her arthritic fingers. "Let me give you a hand with those."

"Thank you. You're such a dear boy. Bless your heart." She patted him on the arm, taking hold of the elbow he held out for her. Lysander assisted her up the sidewalk to the apartment entrance, nodding and smiling as she told him about winning at Bingo the previous day.

Exiting the building, he was still smiling as he flipped the coin Miss Petrie had given him. She always dug to the bottom of her change purse for a quarter for him whenever he helped bring in her groceries. He chuckled. Miss Petrie was one of a kind.

Turning to go left, he barely stopped in time to avoid running into two men standing by the entrance.

"Get out of our way, Null." Crashing against his shoulder as they walked to the door, he was knocked back into the glass.

"Hey, watch it."

One of them turned to him. "Did you say something, freak?"

The other man sneered at Lysander. "Don't talk to the Null. He's too pathetic to waste your breath on." The assholes laughed, fist bumped each other, then walked through the door.

Lysander glared after them. He could hear them snickering about the magicless freak as the door closed. But that was nothing new. Since the day it had been confirmed he didn't possess any magical ability, the entire magical community had looked down on him. His own family, with the exception of his brother, was the worst. Case in point, his two idiot cousins. Thank the Goddess his brother, Bryan, was the Clan leader and made sure everyone knew that Lysander was under his personal protection. It didn't make interactions with them any fun, but it did keep him relatively safe.

Lysander shrugged it off. It had been that way for years. Nothing he did was ever going to change it. He looked down at the quarter clutched in his hand and grinned, bad mood gone. But he could have a cookie with his coffee, compliments of Miss Petrie.

* * *

Sipping his latte, Lysander was unlocking his door when his phone started ringing. Trying to get the door open while answering his phone, juggling his drink, and blocking the opening so his cat didn't escape, was a feat worthy of notice. A quick glance showed the hall was empty of any appreciative audience to see and applaud his amazing agility. He snickered at his foolishness.

By the time he made it inside, the ringing had stopped. Typical. He was just putting his keys on the entryway table when it started ringing again. Checking the display, he frowned. Why was Richie calling this early? As an artist, he usually worked through the night and slept until late morning. Lysander hoped he wasn't canceling their lunch plans. He'd been looking forward to seeing him all week.

"Hey, Richie, what's up?" Sniffling was the only response. Oh Goddess, what now? "What's going on?"

"I need your help." More sniffling.

"Anything." Lysander crossed his fingers, hoping this wasn't what he thought it was, but he was doomed for disappointment.

"I need you to help me move. I'm breaking up with Scott."

Damn it. "What happened? You guys seemed happy." Lysander looked down, distracted when his cat came over to greet him. Jinx wove through his legs, then braced one paw on Lysander's leg and batted at the hem of his shorts. Lysander leaned over and gave him a scratch under his chin, wincing when Jinx's claws flexed, stabbing into his leg.

Breath catching, Richie choked out a watery laugh. "We were happy. But Scott was also happy with Henry, and David, and Matt." There was a pause. "And Jenny."

"Jenny? Really?"

Richie snorted. "Yes. I guess he wanted to experiment. The boy's been gay for almost thirty years and suddenly thinks he needs to try something new. Anyway, I'm out of here. But I could use a hand."

"I'll be right there. Did you need me to grab some boxes?"

"No, I've got enough. But I wouldn't mind a coffee."

"I'll grab one on my way. Try not to smash anything of Scott's before I get there."

"Oops, I probably should have called you sooner. That stupid vase his mother gave him was the first casualty today."

Lysander laughed. "The ugly green one?"

Richie's laughter was good to hear. "Yes, it looks much better in pieces. I swept it into the corner so he could still appreciate it."

Lysander laughed harder. "Best place for it. That ugly green monstrosity should have been kept in the back of the closet and only brought out when his mom dropped by. I never understood why he insisted on displaying it and not your fabulous pieces."

"Me either. But it's not something I have to worry about anymore. Speaking of which, the dragon you commissioned is done. I brought it home from the studio yesterday afternoon so I could give it to you at lunch today. That's how I caught Scott in bed with Henry. He wasn't expecting me back so early." He started sniffing again.

Lysander needed to put a stop to that. Scott definitely wasn't worth it. "I'm on my way right now. While you're waiting, why don't you figure out the next item that might accidentally get dropped out of the window."

Snickering came over the phone. "Okay, Ell. See you soon."

Hanging up, Lysander looked at the ceiling and sighed. Well, crap. There went his plans for the day. He looked mournfully at his drawing table, kissing goodbye to a day of working on his special project.

Lysander looked down at Jinx, who was lying on his foot, chewing his shoelace. "Sorry buddy. Looks like you're on your own for the day" Lysander wiggled his toes to nudge him off. Jinx rolled to his back and started batting at floating dust particles, not upset at all about the change in plans.

* * *

Lysander's feet dragged on his walk home, exhausted from helping Richie move. It had been a day filled with boxes, dust, intermittent crying, followed up by swearing and kicking of things, with the occasional breakable falling out the window. Goddess save him from true love, if such a thing even existed. He had his doubts. After dealing with the aftermath of Richie's breakup all day, he was glad he'd never been brought down by Cupid's arrow. Give him a cat any day. The expectations were very clear; feed it, water it, love it, and in return you may be allowed to pet it, were guaranteed to clean up furballs, and you always woke up with a bum in your face. He snickered. And he wouldn't want it any other way.

Lysander hefted the box holding his new dragon statue—which had been getting heavier the further he walked— into a more comfortable position to ease the strain on his shoulders. Whatever pain he felt was totally worth it. Richie had outdone himself on this piece. And Lysander knew exactly where he was going to put it when he got back to his apartment.

His steps slowed as he reached the last intersection before his street, sure he could feel someone watching him. Looking around, he didn't see anybody, but the sensation of being watched persisted. He quickly crossed the street, then picked up his pace when his building came in sight. Feeling those eyes on him, he sprinted the last few steps and rushed through the door. Pressing his face against the glass, he looked around, but the streets were empty. Nothing was out there. Not even the car that seemed to always be around these days.

Turning away, Lysander headed for the elevators, completely unaware of the shadow on the rooftop across the street watching him.

Chapter Two

"No! I won't do it Mother. I will not marry her. I'm in charge of this clan, not you. You don't have the right to order me to do anything. And I for sure will not be used to fulfill some arrangement you have with one of your cronies. Especially one who's willing to sell off his own daughter to support your personal agenda.

Slap! The sound reverberated through the room as he touched his burning cheek. His angry words stalled when he saw his mother's eyes, the burning fury in them matched only by the iciness of her cold, ruthless heart.

"You listen to me, son." A manicured finger stabbed the air in front of his chest. "You will marry as I say and have an heir to fulfill your duty to this clan, or else."

"Or else what? There is nothing that will make me marry her."

"Is that so?" Seeing the hostile ruthlessness in her eyes, he felt the first stirrings of worry. "Not even to protect your brother?"

* * *

Lysander crashed through the doors of Darkness and slid to a stop, eyes frantically searching the large room. There, in the corner at the end of the bar. Finally, after hours of searching, he'd found him. Making his way across the room, he slid onto the stool beside his older brother. "Bryan, I've been looking everywhere for you." He winced when his brother's red laced eyes landed on him.

"Hey baby bro. Come to congratulate me on my upcoming nuptials?" Bryan raised his pint glass sloppily, beer sloshing over the sides.

"Yeah. What's up with that? Mother's calling everyone and telling them you're marrying Jillian next month. That can't possibly be true."

Gazing into his beer glass, Bryan nodded. "Yep. Mother made me an offer I couldn't refuse."

"Damn that woman. What's she blackmailing you with this time?"

"Nothing for you to worry about, little brother. I'll handle Mother."

"It's me, isn't it?" At Bryan's silence, Lysander was sure of it. "I'm so sorry, Bryan. I hate when she does this."

"Not your fault, Sandi. It is what it is. I'm your big brother. It's my job to protect you."

It was an unfortunate fact that Bryan needed to defend him. His father had died in an accident when Lysander was still a child, so the only one standing between him and his mother's cruelty was Bryan. And she had no qualms about threatening Lysander's well-being to force Bryan to bend to her will.

Lysander folded his arms on the bar and leaned his forehead on them. "I still feel like it's my fault. She wouldn't be this way if the prophecies hadn't been wrong about me having special magical powers. I've tried everything, but I can't find any signs of magic. You know I'd do anything to stop Mother from blackmailing you."

His brother's hand landed on his shoulder. "I know, Sandi. I wish she wasn't like this. A mother should be a mom, not an instrument of terror and manipulation." He patted Lysander, then let his hand drop. "I'm establishing some connections that will help when I'm ready to openly challenge her, but it takes time to build those kinds of alliances. Until then, Mother's sitting in the power seat."

It was a crappy situation. Bryan was in charge of the clan, but had only recently fully taken over. He didn't have the power base his mother had developed over the last century, so she pretty much did whatever she wanted, there not being anyone willing or able to stand against her.

Even moving away from her realm of influence wasn't an option. She had a long reach, so distance was no impediment to her control over Lysander. He'd found that out the hard way when he went to art school. She had connections everywhere who'd had no problem dropping in on Lysander to remind him of how vulnerable he was.

It had improved somewhat since Bryan became head of the clan. He and their mother had developed an uneasy truce; she refrained from harming Lysander and Bryan didn't force the clans to choose between them—mostly because he wasn't sure which way that would go—allowing her to retain much of her control. The part that shamed Lysander the most was the little boy inside of him still hoping for his mommy's love and approval. However, he was slowly coming to the realization that his dreams of that would never come to pass.

Lysander raised his head. "There has to be some way to stop this. I can't let Mother force you to marry Jillian and potentially destroy the rest of your life. We need to stall her until you're ready to challenge her." He sat up straight as a thought crossed his mind. "I can take your place."

"What?" Bryan shook his head. "No. You can't do that. I'll marry Jillian. It's the only way right now."

Lysander turned to him, grasping his arm. "No, it's not. Listen to me. It's the perfect solution." He leaned in closer, speaking firmly. "I know you, Bryan. If you go through with the marriage, you'll feel honor-bound to give it your best effort." He hushed Bryan when he tried to interrupt. "Stop. You know I'm right. If you married her, your integrity would make you stick it out and try to make a real marriage with her." He grabbed Bryan's beer and took a drink, before placing the glass on the far side of himself, out of his brother's reach.

Lysander continued, "Have you even thought about what would happen if you had a kid? You'd never leave your own child, so you'd be stuck with Jillian forever. She's horrible, Bryan. I wouldn't wish her on my worst enemy, never mind subjecting you or a child to her." He leaned back, slapping his hand on the bar top. "I've made my decision. I'm going to take your place."

"Damn it, Sandi. No. I will not let you sacrifice yourself on my behalf."

"But I'm supposed to let you bow to Mother's demands? To keep me safe? No, not a chance. You've been protecting me my whole life. It ends now." Lysander slapped both his hands down on the bar, then stood. "I'm going to go fix this."

He turned to go and crashed into a wall that hadn't been there before. Hands settled on his waist to steady him. Okay then, not a wall. He pressed his hands against the rock-hard chest he was using to steady himself and looked up. Then looked up some more, ending on piercing black eyes. Holy Goddess, this man was truly beautiful. If he had a type, this was definitely it. Too bad about the tiny little detail he'd found out last time; this gorgeous package came with an arrogance to match.

"Careful there, beautiful. We wouldn't want you to fall." That deep, rich voice flowed over him in a caressing wave. His eyes slid closed, savoring the texture. There were more words spoken, many words. In another minute, they'd start making sense. His body unconsciously swayed closer, breathing deep, he inhaled leather and spice, and something else he couldn't place. He took in another lungful. Quiet laughter had his eyes snapping open.

"Smell something you like?"

The screech of a needle on a record sounded in his mind as the spell broke. Lysander pulled his hands away and stepped back. "Nope, not anymore."

"Don't be like that." Hands caught and held Lysander's hand as he moved back, bumping into the barstool behind him. "Please, stay. Come have a drink with me."

Lysander shook his head. "I don't think so." He waved his free hand in front of him. "I'm so over this." He tried to pull his captured hand away but the asshat wouldn't release him. He glared. "Let go of me."

His hand was instantly free. "Sorry, beautiful. I'm making a right mess of this." A hand was held out to him. "Could we perhaps start over? My name is Roman Greystone and this is my place." Lysander just looked at the hand extended to him. It gave a small wiggle. "Don't leave me hanging, beautiful."

Lysander narrowed his eyes. "The name's Lysander. Don't call me beautiful." He reached out and brusquely shook hands. Behind him, he heard banging as Bryan stumbled from his seat.

"Hey, is this dude bothering you, Sandi? Get the hell away from my brother." Bryan came up beside him, glaring belligerently and throwing his chest out.

Lysander snorted. "Way to be on time, big brother." Lysander pushed against his chest. "Go sit down, I've got this handled."

"Are you sure?"

He nodded. "I've got this. Sit. You don't always have to look out for me."

Bryan's arm curled around his neck. "Can't help it. You're my baby brother. I'm always going to have your back, no matter what."

The whiskey smooth voice interrupted. "Gentlemen, please stay. Let me get you both a drink."

"No. I'm leaving." Lysander turned to Bryan. "Did you want to come with me? I'll help get you home."

"Sure."

Lysander wrapped his arm around Bryan's waist, and started to walk, bumping into Roman. Lysander glared. "Excuse us, please." When Roman stepped aside, Lysander helped his brother out of the bar. This time he didn't look back.

"I see that didn't go any better. As a matter of fact, it may have gone worse."

"Shut up, Max."

"Your Bloodmate is a fierce creature."

He was indeed.

* * *

A couple of days later…

Lysander answered the phone, grinning. "Hey, Tommy. How's my cheap-drunk best friend today?" He snorted. "How did I not know this about you?"

"Shut up, Ell. I forgot to eat that day. I was too nervous."

"Uh huh, of course you did." He snickered.

"It's true. Now stop giving me shit."

"Tommy, Tommy, Tommy. I'm your best friend. It's my duty per the friend code to give you as much shit as possible. I figure I can milk this one for years. You know you'd do the same if it had been me."

There was a long pause. "Yeah, you're probably right. Anyway, if you're done amusing yourself at my expense, I called to thank you for getting me home last week."

"No problem. That's what a friend does."

"Did you have time to meet for lunch today? I have a couple of designs I'd like your opinion on."

"Sure. Did you want to meet at the coffee shop?"

"You and your fancy latte fetish. Yes, we can meet there. You're lucky they have awesome sandwiches."

"Never mind my craving for delicious lattes. At least I can drink more than three drinks without thinking I'm Britney."

"Shut up."

Lysander laughed when Tommy hung up on him.

* * *

Lysander leaned back in his chair and looked out the window while he sipped his latte. There. It was the car that had been following him all week. He only caught a glimpse as it passed by, but he would swear it was the same one.

"Are you even listening to me?"

Oops, he was now. "Sorry, Tommy. I thought I saw something."

"You've been distracted since we got here. What's going on?"

Lysander took in the concerned expression on his friend's face, wondering how much to share. Taking another sip of his latte to give himself a moment to think, he decided to go all in. Tommy was his best friend.

"Mother's stirring up trouble again. I'm working on a plan to protect Bryan and me, but Mother has a way of screwing everything up."

"Sometimes I really hate your mother."

"Me too, Tommy."

"Is that it? Because your mother is always up to something. This feels like something else."

Lysander paused. "I think someone's following me."

Tommy's eyes widened. "Really? Why would anybody be following you?"

"I have no idea. But I keep seeing the same car everywhere I go."

"Are you sure it's the same one. It's not like you're a car guy or anything. It could be a coincidence."

"How many black, chauffeur driven cars, with tinted windows, do you see driving around our neighborhood?"

Tommy squinted. "Huh. Well, when you put it like that, none really."

"I know. It's driving me crazy. I can't see who's in the back and there's no reason for anybody to follow me."

"All you can do is keep a close eye out and call your brother or me if anything hinky happens. I'll watch too." He thought for a moment. "Do you think this has anything to do with your mother?"

"I wouldn't put it past her." Lysander drank the last of his latte, keeping one eye on the activities outside the coffee shop. His mother? Perhaps. It just didn't feel like her. This was something else.

* * *

"I'm telling you, Bryan. Either someone is following me or I'm losing my mind." Lysander braced the phone between his shoulder and cheek as he unlocked the door. Gently pushing Jinx back as he walked in, he closed the door, setting the bag of cat food beside it. "It's really freaking me out. The same car is always driving around wherever I go during the day. It never stops, just drives past me. And when I'm out at night, I can feel someone watching me, but again, there's never anybody there."

Lysander walked across the room and sat on the couch, kicking off his shoes and stretching out with his feet on the coffee table. "You think it could be stress? Really?" He shook his head, "I don't think so. Stress doesn't make you think the boogieman is following you." He rubbed Jinx's belly when the cat flopped down beside him, a claw digging into his hand in return. "Changing the subject, have you heard from Mother lately? No? Me either. That kind of worries me."

He got up, grabbed the bag of food he'd left by the door, and headed to the kitchen, followed by a very vocal Jinx. "That sound? That's Jinx wanting his dinner. Stop laughing. He's not a devil cat; he's just a misunderstood angel." He glared down at his angel when he got a swipe of claws across his ankle for being too slow in putting out the food.

"Sure, we can meet up for a drink. Just let me finish feeding your furry nephew and I'll head out. Darkness? Are you sure you want to go back there? I thought maybe we could try a new place." Lysander raised his eyes skyward, mouthing please. "No. No reason. We can meet there if you want." He nodded. "All right, Bryan, see you in an hour or so." He ended the call.

Darkness. Absolutely the last place he wanted to go.

Chapter Three

Max appeared in his doorway. "He's back."

Roman quickly got up from behind his desk, tugged on his cuffs, then ran a hand through his hair, straightening the long strands.

"Do you really think it's going to make any difference how your hair looks? *Sorry, mate. I didn't mean to offend you the last time we met. Look at my beautiful hair and forgive me.*" Max laughed. "I don't think the way you look is the problem. Perhaps you should try being less of an arrogant ass."

"I beg your pardon. Me, arrogant?" Max just raised his eyebrow in response. Roman rolled his eyes. "Perhaps you have a point. I do seem to have a talent for antagonizing my Bloodmate. I will try to be more gracious." When Max continued to look at him, Roman sighed. "And be less of an ass."

"That's the spirit." Max slapped him on the back. "Now go get your man."

Sometimes he wondered why he kept Max around.

Roman paused just out of earshot, or rather, human earshot, and shamelessly listened in on his Bloodmate's conversation.

"I've been giving it a lot of thought, and it's the only way, Bryan. No, hear me out. You need time to establish yourself. If I take your place, I can give you that time. Besides, nobody's ever going to want me since I don't have magic. This is really the best solution."

Roman stared longingly at his Bloodmate, thinking, I want you. And he did. Roman was very pleased with the Goddess who had blessed him with a truly exceptional mate whose big heart cared deeply for others. He was also a joy to look at from his short, dark brown hair with red highlights, to his elegant features, a hidden dimple he wanted to see directed his way, and open smiling face. His mate would fool many into thinking he was easy-going but Roman had felt the feisty man's bite. He knew of the fire hiding within him.

Roman tore his gaze off his mate when the other man started to speak, realizing something important was going on.

"There has to be a better way, Lysander."

"Uh, oh. You're using my full name."

"That's because I don't want you to do this."

"I have to, Bryan. I've been a burden on you long enough. But don't worry. I think I've come up with a way where we both win."

"How?"

"I don't want to say anything until I have a chance to speak with Mother."

"I think this is a big mistake, Sandi."

"So, you've said. But it's mine to make, big brother. Now, I'm done with this discussion. Why don't you tell me why you like coming here? You do realize the place is filled with vampires, right?"

"Darkness caters to all paranormal types, not just vampires. That's why I come here. I can relax and be myself and not have to worry about dealing with humans."

"I see humans in the crowd though. Quite a lot of them. The vampires are snacking on them."

Bryan laughed. "I know. Many of the humans that come here do so specifically for the bite. It's supposed to be quite exhilarating."

"Huh, I don't know that I'd want a vampire using me for a chew toy."

Roman smiled to himself. *You have so much to learn, my precious Bloodmate.* Realizing this was as good a time as any to interrupt, Roman stopped by their table. "Good evening gentlemen."

Two pairs of eyes turned to him, one polite and questioning, one annoyed and glaring. Roman sighed inwardly. *His Bloodmate, always so difficult.*

"Sorry to interrupt, but I have something to discuss that might be of interest to you both."

"What makes you think we'd be interested in anything you have to say?" Though his words were hostile, Lysander's body leaned toward him. Roman could see the fight in his eyes between his instincts that were urging him closer to his fated mate and his desire to push Roman away. *His Bloodmate's strength would stand him in good stead when they Bonded.*

"I overheard some of your discussion and I might have a solution to what appears to be an untenable situation?"

"What the hell man?" Bryan banged his glass on the table, "That was a private conversation."

"Yeah, we were speaking quietly. How could you possibly have overheard us?"

Roman leaned closer. "Perhaps to a human you were quiet, but as I'm not human, I heard you quite clearly. No conversation is really private to me, especially in my own place." He straightened. "For the sake of your privacy, perhaps we should continue this discussion in my office. Or if you prefer, we could go to my private suite on the upper level."

"You live above the bar?"

"Yes. My staff also have accommodations on site, which can be part of our discussion once we are in a secure location."

The brothers looked at each other. Lysander's head cocked, Bryan's eyebrow raised, Lysander's head tilted the other way, Bryan's mouth pursed. Roman was amused, watching an entire conversation taking place without a word being said.

Eventually they reached an agreement. "Fine. We'll come to your office, but I want an explanation about the not human part." Lysander stood from his chair and waited for Bryan to join him.

"Absolutely. This way gentlemen." Roman led them through an opening off to one side of the bar, down a long hallway, ending in front of a solid oak door. He opened it, ushering them inside.

Roman swallowed a sigh of relief at finally getting a chance to explain. After one thousand years of searching, after losing all hope, he had finally found the other half of his soul. It was exhilarating on one hand and terrifying on the other. Especially since he'd managed to offend his mate from their very first meeting, and every time he opened his mouth thereafter. The upcoming conversation would be tricky to navigate without further damaging his image in his mate's eyes. Sending a quick prayer to the Goddess for inspiration, he followed the men into his office, locking the door behind him.

The two men seated themselves in front of his large mahogany desk. Roman walked around to the other side and sat in his custom-made black leather chair. Placing his elbows on the desk, Roman linked his fingers and stared at them, wondering where to begin. When they began shifting uncomfortably under his intense scrutiny, he leaned back in his chair.

"Let me be frank, gentlemen. I've lived a very long time and believe in direct and clear conversation, without worrying about social niceties and political correctness. I don't intend to change." Roman shot a meaningful glance over to Lysander, who looked confused. No matter, he would understand shortly. "I'll get right to the point." Roman nodded at Bryan, "Regardless of your personal shielding, I can tell you are a magic user and a very powerful one. I suspect you are a leader to your clan."

Bryan reared back in his chair. "What? You shouldn't be able to tell that."

Roman turned to his mate. "But you puzzle me. While you are not registering to my senses as a magic user, I am picking up something unusual about you." Roman tilted his head, contemplating the surprised man. "I cannot quite put my finger on what it is."

Lysander snorted, his lips turning downward. "Probably because I'm what everyone refers to as a Null. As in I have no magic. Ergo, I'm of no use to anyone." Bitterness filled his words.

Bryan grabbed his arm and squeezed gently. "You're my baby brother and you're everything to me." Lysander nodded, but Roman noticed the sadness stayed in his eyes.

Bryan turned to Roman. "Now tell me who or what the hell you are and how you know these things?' He paused "And also why your staff live here, which is a bit unorthodox."

"Of course." Roman smiled sharply. He raised his hands, palms up, and gestured as though he was introducing the next item up for bid. "As I mentioned the other day, I own Darkness. I also own the rest of the building and the surrounding block"

Lysander rolled his eyes. "How wonderful for you."

Holding back a smile at his mate's cheek, Roman continued. "As for how I can sense what you are, I am a vampire. In fact, I am the leader of all covens in North America. Most of my staff are coven members. They live in the building as this is our home."

"Impossible." Bryan stood forcefully from his chair. "I know there are many vampires at this club. That's why I frequent the place. But you, sir, are not. If you were a vampire, I would be able to sense it."

"Would you now?" Roman smirked.

"Yes, I would. I am Bryan Galway IV, preeminent magic user of Clan Galway, and will be appointed as the next Council member upon my thirtieth birthday.

Lysander snorted, face-palming. "Dear Goddess, Bryan. Could you sound any more pompous?"

"I could."

"That was rhetorical."

Bryan punched his shoulder casually, still keeping a close eye on Roman.

Roman watched the byplay with some amusement. "If I might continue?"

Bryan nodded, glowering as he retook his seat.

"Your ability to sense the younger vampires is expected in such a powerful magic user. However, after a thousand years, I have learned how to mask my powers from other paranormal groups. It helps keep my coven safe from those who would otherwise challenge me, wanting to make a name for themselves. Observe." Roman relaxed the rigid hold he had on himself, which was necessary to control his powerful nature. He allowed himself a tiny smirk at Bryan's shock upon feeling the full strength of his power.

"Holy shit." Bryan looked at Lysander, "He's not kidding. He's got turbo-charged super vampire mojo."

"Super vampire mojo? That's the scientific term for it, Mr. Preeminent magic user?" Lysander snarked at him. There was no response as Bryan was still looking at Roman in awe. Lysander eventually rolled his eyes and turned to Roman. "Fine. We've established that you're the big kahuna vampire. Why are we here?"

Moment of truth. Hoping this conversation didn't go sideways, Roman tipped his head to Lysander. "You are the one I have been searching for my entire adult life. You are my Bloodmate, as gifted to me by the Goddess herself."

"What?" Lysander started shaking his head. "No, that's impossible."

"I assure you, it is very possible."

"No, you must be joking," Lysander denied. "I can't be your mate, or Bloodmate, or whatever."

Roman was devastated by his mate's reaction, but hid it, taking a moment to clarify. "It's Bloodmate formally, though also referred to as mate or Bonded, when the joining is complete. And I am quite serious as I have been looking for my Bloodmate for almost one thousand years. I would not kid about this."

Bryan jumped from his chair again. "A mating between you is forbidden. The Council has stated that magic users cannot bond with another paranormal. Magic users can only bond with other magic users or humans. Breaking the law is punishable by death. Sandi cannot be your Bloodmate. I will not allow it."

Roman rose from his chair, slamming his hands down on his desk. "He is my mate," he roared. "Mine!" Roman deliberately pushed power over Bryan, taking satisfaction in the fear that filled the magic user's face. Bryan fell back into his chair. "Nobody will interfere in my bonding; do you understand me?" Roman's rage grew at the thought of anything threatening his mate. "Mine," he said again, hissing through his teeth that had elongated in his anger. He pushed more power out, until Bryan curled in on himself.

Roman eventually became aware of hands gently patting his chest. The red haze cleared from his vision.

"It's okay, big guy. Bryan didn't mean to threaten you." Lysander pushed him back into his chair, his hands stroking soothingly down Roman's arms. "I think he understands now," Lysander soothed. "Perhaps you could pull back some on the power blast."

Right, that. Roman closed his eyes and tried to clamp down on his power. When that didn't work, he focused on his mate's soothing presence, breathing him in deep. After a few moments, he finally regained his lost control and locked down on his powers.

"That's better. Even the red has left your eyes now." Lysander patted his shoulder.

"My eyes turned red?" Roman turned to Bryan. "You are fortunate to be alive. Red eyes mean I am at my most dangerous. It's only a short step to turning feral if I don't regain control of myself. You can thank your brother for saving your life." Roman looked at Lysander. "Thank you, I'm good now." He patted Lysander's hand, then clasped it between both of his. "Truly, I thank you. I wouldn't have wanted to hurt you by killing your brother. As your mate, my strongest desire is to make you happy."

Lysander avoided his eyes. "Yeah, about that. I can't be your mate." He winced when Roman's hands involuntarily squeezed his trapped hand. "Maybe you should let me go so I can sit down and explain."

Roman loosened his grip, but shook his head. He pulled one hand away and patted his lap, "You can sit here while we discuss this."

Lysander raised an eyebrow at this suggestion. "I don't think so." He leaned against the desk "I'll just stand here."

"It was worth a try." Roman shrugged, then turned serious. "Please explain why you do not want to be my mate."

"It's not that I don't want to. It's just—" Lysander inhaled deeply, air gusting as he breathed out. "I'm not sure how much you overheard from our conversation. In a nutshell, Bryan is being forced to marry another clan leader's daughter. Our mother is power-hungry and driven to obtain a seat on the Council, at any cost. She's made a pact for alliance with this other clan, through Bryan's marriage. Once Mother has a strong enough power base, she plans to overthrow the current Elders and rule the Council herself."

"I see. What does that have to do with our mating?"

"Mother is making threats against me to force Bryan to cooperate. Since I have no power of my own, Bryan has always had to protect me from her power games. This is just one more time where my weakness is being used against him, and I can't let him do it." Lysander turned to Bryan. "I just can't. Enough is enough. It's not fair to you, Bryan."

"Sandi, it doesn't matter if it's fair. I only want what's best for you. You're my brother. I love you."

"I love you, too. That's why it's time for me to have your back." Lysander turned to Roman, his eyes glinting. "I'm sorry, Roman. For his whole life," he said quietly, "Bryan has made sacrifices to keep me safe. I won't let him do it again."

"My poor mate," Roman said, cupping his face. "I can protect you from her."

Lysander shook his head. "I can't take that chance. You don't understand how vicious Mother can be or how many people she can call upon." Lysander blinked, clearing the moisture from his eyes. "I have to take Bryan's place, until he has time to build a strong enough power base to challenge Mother."

"Lysander, no." Bryan rushed over. "You need to reconsider. A mating is everything, even if it is forbidden." He looked worriedly at Roman when he growled. "I'll work on changing that rule once I'm on the Council. Until then, I will protect you both from any repercussions from them."

"No, Bryan. This is one time I can protect you and nothing will stop me." Lysander looked at Roman. "You are beyond beautiful and very strong." He tapped his chest. "I'm drawn to you already and I can feel that I'm hurting you. We just met at the wrong time." He curled his hand over his heart. "I'm so very sorry for causing you pain, but I can't be your mate."

His face clouded with distress, Lysander stood up from the desk, dodging as Roman reached for him, and rushed for the door. "You deserve so much better than this, Roman. I wish you hadn't been matched with me."

"Lysander, stop. Please," Roman cried out imploringly, reaching toward him as he fled.

The slamming door underscored the finality of his mate's words.

Chapter Four

Lysander paced across the floor of his mother's study, nervously wiping his sweaty palms on his pants. According to the housekeeper, his mother would be with him shortly. Which was a good thing as his anxiousness grew with every minute that passed. Part of it was because of the room. It had been years since he'd last been in it and he hadn't missed it in the slightest.

In his agitation, it took some time before he noticed the changes his mother had made.

The comfortable chairs had been replaced by elegant pieces that looked as if they'd collapse if anyone larger than a child sat in them. They also didn't look very comfortable. He walked over and carefully perched on one of the chairs in front of his mother's desk to verify. Yep. Elegant and hard. Kind of like his mother. He'd definitely be standing for today's meeting.

Wandering over to the shelves, he was saddened to see she'd removed all pictures of his father and any mementos of his and Bryan's childhood. The spaces had been filled with crystal prism ornaments; elegant and beautiful, but impersonal. He went over to the French doors and parted the coverings to let in the sun, pleased at the resulting colorful arrays when the beams of light were dispersed through the prisms. It was the only color in the otherwise austere and cold room. He sighed as he looked around. The room was a clear representation of the condition of his mother's heart, icy cold and inhospitable.

Glancing at his watch, he was surprised to see he'd been waiting over thirty minutes. Lysander hoped his mother would show up soon as he was already second guessing his decision. His head knew this was the right thing to do, but his heart wouldn't let him forget the devastation on Roman's face. How he could feel such heartache for a man he barely knew was bewildering, but it suggested he might be making a mistake. Bryan certainly thought so. Perhaps he should go. No, Bryan was the reason he was doing this; he owed it to him.

Lysander pressed a hand to his chest, sure he could feel Roman's pain. Was that the bond? Dear Goddess. If it was, he was so wrong. He couldn't do this to Roman. Bryan would forgive him if he chose his mate over him. He was sure of it.

Lysander turned to the door, ready to bolt, when it opened and his mother glided into the room. It was too late to back out now.

Lysander stood motionless in the center of the room as Charlotte gracefully sat in the velvet covered chair behind the antique Victorian walnut desk and began going through the stack of messages that had been left there. Not once did she acknowledge Lysander's presence. And he knew better than to interrupt her. She'd let him know when she was ready to speak with him. He rolled his eyes internally. There were always power games in play when dealing with his mother.

After letting him stew for another fifteen minutes, Charlotte finally gave him her attention, her pale blue eyes glinting like frozen ice crystals. Lysander couldn't recall a time when his mother had looked at him with anything other than disdain.

"Why are you here wasting my time? Surely you've accomplished nothing important enough to interrupt my day." Charlotte peered at her nails, before glancing his way. "Well? Speak up. I have more important things to attend to than waiting for you to get to the point."

"Why, I'm fine. Thank you for asking. And a very pleasant morning to you as well, Mother." Sarcasm was a bad choice, but it was a conditioned response when dealing with Charlotte.

"You have ten minutes before my next appointment. So please, do carry on wasting my time."

"Fine." Lysander moved to lean on the front of her desk, hoping he was leaving his handprints on the highly polished surface. "I want to take Bryan's place and marry Jillian."

"You?" Charlotte sniffed. "In what way could you possibly take your brother's place? He at least has power to offer. You are useless and bring nothing of value to the table."

Lysander flinched before he could stop it. "I wish you could find something in me to love. It's not normal for a mother to hate her own son the way you do me."

"And I wish you had the powers you were prophesied to have; yet here we are."

Even after being slighted his entire life, his mother's words still had the power to hurt. Lysander worked hard not to show her barb had found its mark. "That may be,

Mother, but perhaps my child will prove to be more powerful than I."

"Your child."

"Yes. Mine when I marry Jillian."

Charlotte studied at him a moment before she tilted her head, clearly intrigued. "I'm listening."

Lysander braced himself. Here went nothing. "I'm offering to marry Jillian in Bryan's place. Once my child is born and shows that he or she has a magical signature, I'll have the marriage dissolved. You'll have the powerful child of prophecy you've always wanted and Bryan and I will finally be done with you."

Charlotte peered down her nose at him. "What in the world makes you think I would agree to such terms? As it stands now, I control Bryan through you and can make him marry Jillian. Really, your only value to me is as a tool to ensure your brother does as I wish."

Ouch, that stung. Lysander forced a laugh, even though this situation was anything but funny. "Here's the thing, Mother. A small detail you may have overlooked." He paused for effect…and let's face it, the annoyance factor. "Good luck in getting a child from Bryan."

"He'll do as he's told."

"You really think so? Perhaps you've forgotten Bryan told you he was gay when he was fifteen. I'm pretty sure Jillian will have a hard time, well, getting him hard." Lysander's inner man-child snickered at his own words.

His mother, on the other hand, was not amused. "There's no need to be crass. It shows poor breeding."

"Really? That shows poor breeding? A spot of blackmail before breakfast; no problem. Threatening and abusing your own children to strengthen your power base; bonus points. Risqué word-play; bzzzt. Nope. That's not allowed and shows poor taste." Lysander didn't expect her to acknowledge his words, so wasn't surprised when she ignored his outburst.

"Your brother knows his duty to the clan. He'll do as I say."

Lysander had to laugh. "Good Goddess. It doesn't work that way Mother. Not even for you. If you force this marriage, you'll get nothing out of it. Imagine how embarrassed you'll be when your own progeny can't impregnate your hand-picked broodmare to produce the next great mage."

That got her attention, perhaps too well. "Be very careful how you speak to me, child."

Webs of power wrapped around him with squeezing pressure. He fought hard not to show any distress, but it got more difficult to breathe the longer she held him. He glared at her to no effect. Eventually she released him, allowing him to take a deep, gasping breath.

"Overlooking your poor manners, you may have a point." Charlotte smiled viciously at him.

As Lysander struggled to get his breathing under control, it was dawning on him that he might have made a huge mistake in coming here. He should have known better than to try and make a deal with the devil. Unfortunately, he was in too deep to get out safely now. There was nothing to do but push through to the end and hope he survived.

"Let us be very clear on what you're offering," Charlotte said, folding her hands on her desk. "You will take your brother's place and marry Jillian. You will do this without being difficult and will produce a child as quickly as possible."

"Yes."

She paused, then struck again. "What if the child turns out to be as useless as you? What then?"

"I doubt that will be the case," Lysander said. "The seers predicted that the greatest power of this century would come from me. Since I don't have any power myself, it stands to reason it will be my child who will fulfill the prophecy." Lysander stepped back from the desk. "My offer is that when this magical child is born, I'm free to leave Jillian, dissolving all ties to both her and the child. I'll have fulfilled any possible obligations you seem to think are due, and you and I will be done."

Charlotte looked thoughtful. Lysander waited as she considered his offer, trying not to fidget. Surreptitiously, he looked at the desktop and held back a grin. A perfect set of handprints marred the pristine shine his mother insisted on. It was petty of him to enjoy how much it would annoy her, but that was how their relationship worked.

After a few moments, Charlotte's laser sharp gaze focused on him. "I will let Jillian's father know you will be taking your brother's place in uniting our clans. I can't risk Bryan failing in his husbandly duties." Charlotte reached for her phone. "I have arrangements to make. Be here next month, the third Saturday, at noon." Charlotte began dialing, one eyebrow lifting as she glanced up, as though surprised to see him still standing there. "You're dismissed."

Lysander snorted. "One day you'll regret the way you treat me."

"But it will not be this day," Charlotte said, not looking up from her phone.

She never gave an inch. "I'll show myself out." Striding from the room, he had a momentary thought as to how easy it had been to make that deal. He stumbled. It had been easy. Far too easy. Damn it. What trap had he just climbed into?

* * *

Lysander was startled out of a sound sleep by loud banging on his door. Pushing Jinx aside, he checked the time. Oh, hell no, it was way too early for visitors. The banging started again. Groaning, Lysander fell back against the bed and pulled a pillow over his head hoping to drown out the noise.

Sleep was just pulling him back into its comforting arms when his phone began ringing with his brother's imperious ringtone. He ignored it until it stopped. Then there was more banging. "Sandi, I know you're in there. Open up before I kick this door in.." His phone started ringing again.

"For the love of…" Lysander rolled out of bed, tossing his pillow against the wall. He stomped to the door, Jinx following along, meowing loudly at his side. Wrenching open the door, Lysander narrowly missed getting knocked in the face by Bryan's fist. "Do you have any idea what time it is?"

"Sandi, I need—"

"No." He slammed the door in his brother's face.

Bryan knocked again, quieter but no less demanding. "Lysander, we need to talk." Great. Now Bryan was using his full name. He only pulled that out when shit was about to get real.

Sighing, Lysander opened the door again. "What is so important you had to wake me up in the middle of the night?"

Bryan snorted, pushing past him. "Hardly the middle of the night." Walking into the kitchen, he started making a pot of coffee. Good, maybe he wouldn't have to kill his brother. At least, not until he'd had his first cup. "Why are you still in bed anyway? It's almost noon."

"Why are you an asshole?" Lysander muttered under his breath. Closing the door firmly, okay, slamming it—the neighbors were up now anyway—Lysander joined his brother in the kitchen and stood in front of the coffee machine, waiting impatiently for the slowly brewing, life affirming, morning gift from the gods. He reached out blindly to grasp the empty mug Bryan handed to him. "Thanks."

Bryan laughed. "I'll wait until you're more civilized, then we can talk." He checked out the cat yowling by Lysander's feet. "What's wrong with your cat?"

Lysander looked down at his dramatically wailing cat, then at Bryan, then back to the coffee that was almost finished brewing, and shrugged. "Nothing."

"Are you sure? It sounds possessed."

"He is not an it, and he is apparently starving, even though I fed him a few hours ago." Lysander poured himself a cup of coffee, closing his eyes as he brought it to his mouth, breathing in the fresh-brewed aroma, then practically inhaled the whole cup in one go. If he had to deal with his brother this early in the day, he would need the hit of caffeine.

Jinx's continued wails finally reached his nerve endings. "Good Goddess, you sound like you're dying, Jinx. Give me a second." Deciding to go with speed over gourmet wet food, he opened the cupboard and scooped out a cup of kibble from the bag, dumping it into his devil cat's dish. Jinx quickly pounced on it like it might escape. Ahh, the silence was beautiful. Too bad Bryan had to ruin it.

"I want to talk to you."

"About?"

"I want to talk about Mother and this upcoming marriage."

"Nope, that subject is closed. Next." Lysander poured another coffee and took a seat at the table. Bryan joined him.

"Let's reopen it."

"No. Move on, Bryan."

"Lysander, listen to me. I can't let you walk away from your mate. Do you even understand how rare it is to find that one special person gifted to you by the Goddess? You don't turn your back on that."

"I thought it was forbidden."

"That doesn't change how rare and special it is."

"I know." Lysander sighed and leaned against his brother's shoulder. "All my life you've sacrificed and protected me from Mother or anyone else who tried to use me or hurt me. You've made it your mission to keep me safe. And I appreciate everything you've done for me." Lysander set down his empty cup and reached for his brother's hand. "But it's time for me to protect you. I can't do much, but this, I can. Besides," Lysander braced himself, "I've already spoken with Mother."

"Damn it, Sandi. Why didn't you wait?"

"I thought I had a solid plan. Something she wouldn't be able to say no to."

"And?"

"She's agreed to let me take your place, so everything's fine." Lysander waited. His brother was no dummy.

"What else did you have to agree to? No way did Mother just accept switching grooms."

"Firstborn child," Lysander mumbled.

"What was that?"

Lysander glared at him. "I said, firstborn child." He quickly explained when the color drained from Bryan's face. "I had no choice. Mother needed something more and once I pointed out you wouldn't be able to produce any offspring and her only option was me, she agreed."

"You are no more able to have a child with Jillian than I am. Why would she agree to that?"

"Probably because she doesn't care enough to know anything about me."

"Sandi—"

"Don't. I know I keep hoping Mother will change, but I'm not stupid. I know it's not going to happen." Lysander got up and pulled a package of pre-cooked bacon and a dozen eggs from the refrigerator, then set a pan on the burner to heat up. "I told her we were done with her once the child showed signs of magic and she agreed."

Bryan shook his head. "And you actually believed her? Oh, Sandi, like she'd ever let us escape her clutches. Not while she still has use for us."

"Yeah, so about that." Lysander cleared his throat. "Mother agreed way too easily to my suggestion. I fell right into her trap. We're going to need to let this play out so you know what we're dealing with." He laid strips of bacon in the heating pan.

"You still can't marry Jillian. You definitely can't have a child with her."

"Uh, gay, remember? There will be no child. And you know I have to marry Jillian to spring Mother's trap. You still need time to build your alliances so you can challenge her. This is the only way to give you that."

"And what about your mate? Where's Roman in all these plans of yours?"

Lysander looked away from the bacon frying in the pan. "Bryan, I have no choice. It's either you or me. How can I possibly be happy bonding with Roman knowing the price you'll have to pay?"

"How am I supposed to live with myself knowing what you sacrificed for my freedom?"

That was a great question. To give himself time to come up with an answer his brother would accept, Lysander lifted the cooked bacon from the pan onto a paper towel covered plate. Cracking eggs into the pan, he said quietly, "I guess I'm hoping Roman will wait for me. That he won't hate me too much for not putting him first. When this is over, I'd like to get to know him better and see if he still wants to bond with me." He paused. "That is, if he can forgive me."

When the eggs finished cooking, he placed them on two plates, split the bacon evenly, then set the plates on the table. Grabbing utensils, he joined Bryan and started eating, even though he'd lost his appetite. "Please accept my decision, Bryan. This is hard enough. I don't want to fight with you as well."

"Oh, Sandi." Bryan wrapped him up in a tight hug. "I think you're making the wrong choice, but I'll respect your wishes. I love you, baby brother. I just want you to be happy and safe."

Lysander sniffed, his voice cracking as he spoke, "We might just have to hope for safe. I think the happy ship has sailed." Bryan squeezed him tighter. "Eat, before it gets cold."

Digging in, Bryan ate a couple of bites, then paused. Pointing his fork, he asked, "Does he have to do that when I'm eating?"

Looking in the direction he was pointing, Lysander chuckled. Jinx was on the back of the couch, just a few feet from where they sat eating. His leg was stretched over his head as he bent himself in half to lick around his tail. "He's just cleaning himself. All cats do it."

Bryan whined, "But I'm eating. Does he have to do it here?"

"It's his house. He can do whatever he wants."

"Why is he taking so long?" Bryan whined.

Lysander pushed his plate away, giving up on choking anything down, and forced a grin. "If you could lick your own ass, I'm sure you'd be very thorough with it too." He laughed when Bryan glared and punched him in the arm.

The punch may have hurt, but the laughter soothed his aching heart.

Chapter Five

Someone knocked on his apartment door as Lysander was putting the finishing touches on the charcoal sketch he was working on for his brother. "It's Grand Central Station around here today," Lysander muttered, wiping his hands off on his pants as he walked to the door. Peering through the peephole he saw Roman. He quickly opened the door.

"Roman. What are you doing here?" Lysander stood a moment, drinking in the sight of the vampire who was totally rocking the Goth look today. Full-length black leather jacket, fitted black dress shirt, tailored pants, and black leather boots. Lysander's greedy eyes roamed from head to toe and back, pausing on Roman's dark sapphire eyes. They were sapphire, not black, as he'd thought. Lysander sighed. Between the long black hair, mysterious dark eyes, and the amazingly beautiful physique clothed in black leather, the man was a rock god.

"Ahem."

Oops. Lysander looked up, grinning sheepishly at Roman. "Sorry about that. Well, not really, but whatever." He shrugged.

"Won't you invite me in?" Roman asked.

"Yes, of course. Please come in." Lysander stood off to the side, leaving space for him to enter. Closing the door behind Roman, he asked, "So, it's true what they say then? Vampires can't come in unless invited?"

Roman laughed. "No. It is good manners to wait until you are invited in. Hollywood has much to answer for concerning people's misconceptions about vampires as most of what they portray has little in common with reality." Taking off his coat, Roman laid it over the back of the couch, then gazed around the apartment, his eyes moving over Lysander's comfortable, earth-tone furniture, his picture covered walls, stopping momentarily on his collection of eclectic mythical statues, before he nodded approvingly. "You have a lovely home, Lysander. Are those your work?" he asked, indicating the pictures on the walls.

"The drawings, yes. The statues are from a sculptor friend of mine, Richie. I love his fantasy-themed pieces."

Roman walked closer to look at a dragon statue. Lysander saw the moment he noticed the drawing on the wall and the confused expression on his face as he leaned in, studying the picture intently. Finally, Roman spoke. "At first, I thought this was Bryan, but this man's eyes are filled with anger, something I cannot envision seeing in your overprotective brother. He also appears older. Not physically, but it shows in his eyes, as if he had experienced much hardship in his life."

"That's my father. I had to draw it from memory since he died when I was nine," Lysander said softly. "The last time I saw him, he was fighting with Mother. I don't remember what the fight was about, but I remember how his face looked."

"I'm sorry you lost him." Roman gently touched his cheek with his fingertips. "Especially when you were so young."

"Thanks." Lysander looked around, biting his top lip. "Did you want to sit?" He motioned between the chair and couch.

"Yes, thank you." Roman settled down on the couch, patting the cushion beside him. "Come, Lysander. Sit, so we can get to know one another better."

Shaking off the poignant mood that thoughts of his father always brought, Lysander deliberately sat in the chair, raising an eyebrow in defiance as he prepared for Roman's response. Roman quirked an eyebrow, but let it go.

Jinx chose that moment to stroll out of the bedroom. The moment he saw the vampire in his territory, his ears flattened, his tail lashed, and he started a growling hiss that Lysander had never heard from him before. Roman watched intently for a moment, then bared his fangs and hissed back. Jinx screeched a howling meow and bolted back to the bedroom.

"Was that really necessary?"

"Alpha rules." Apparently Roman didn't feel any shame for terrorizing his poor cat.

Lysander shook his head at the unrepentant vampire. "Can you tell me more about vampires and what Hollywood got wrong?"

"Of course," Roman said, though he looked puzzled. "Do magic users not teach their young about the other paranormal communities?"

"I'm sure most of them do. But if you have no magic and a mother like mine, that becomes privileged information. Since I never hung out with any other paranormals, it wasn't worth going behind her back to find anything out." He shrugged. "I spent most of my childhood and teen years hiding from her and focusing on my art anyway."

"I see. Then here is your first lesson in Vampire 101." Roman started ticking items off on his fingers. "As we have already discussed, vampires do not need an invitation to go anywhere. Not even into a church. They do not burst into flames, regardless of what the priests would have you believe."

Lysander laughed at his dry tone.

Smiling, Roman continued. "It is true that a vampire cannot walk in direct sunlight, though the very oldest can stand a few moments at dawn and dusk without harm. A vampire is also immortal in the sense that we are very long lived. However, we can be killed." He looked at Lysander. "Perhaps it is best if I keep the ways of that to myself until we get to know each other better. I seem to have a talent for making you angry."

Lysander snorted, thinking that was probably a good idea.

His eyes sparkling, Roman said, "We are born, not turned, nor can we turn anyone else. We can eat food, as you do, though vampires do require fresh blood to survive as it holds essential nutrients that our bodies are unable to obtain from meat or other food sources. Though I will admit to enjoying a good steak every once in a while."

Lysander was fascinated. "Do you have to drink human blood?"

"No. We can get what we need from animal sources as well, but human blood is richer and more flavorful." He kissed his fingertips, startling a laugh out of Lysander.

"What else?"

Roman's face got more serious. "Vampires can turn feral if they have gone too long without feeding. If they cannot be brought back soon enough, they have to be put down or they become insanely angry and destructive. That is where Hollywood got the idea of out of control, murdering beasts. We are actually quite civilized."

Seeing the manner in which Roman conducted himself, Lysander could easily believe that. But he wanted to know more. Questions flew out of his mouth rapid-fire "Can you fly or turn into a bat? Do you fade into mist or do you just turn invisible? Can you entrance people?"

Roman laughed. "No, no, no, no, and not quite."

"How so?" Lysander tilted his head, confused when Roman began fidgeting uneasily. Suspicion dawned in his mind. "Roman, what's going on?"

"Well, a vampire cannot entrance anyone per se; however, he can push for certain emotions."

"Like?" He asked slowly, his suspicions definitely growing.

"Things like fear, cooperation, enjoyment, fatigue, passion. It is to help with feeding, you understand. It is much more enjoyable to eat if your host is having fun rather than screaming in terror."

"Okay, I can see that. Can you force these feelings?"

"No. It is more of a suggestion. A vampire can push for certain feelings, but there is always the option to say no and walk away." He cleared his throat. "Unless of course, the vampire is older. Power increases with age, as do inherent abilities, so an older vampire will have greater powers of persuasion. But they still do not have the ability to make you do something against your will."

"I see." Lysander frowned. "Did you use your powers on me?"

Roman looked a bit embarrassed. "I might have done so, yes." He held his hands up when Lysander scowled at him. "Only the first time we met. You intrigued me and I wanted to talk to you. To get to know you. However, once I realized you were my Bloodmate, I stopped. I would not use my abilities on you. I was rather hoping you would feel the pull of the mating bond." Roman smiled fondly at Lysander. "I did not realize at the time how strong your powers of resistance were."

Lysander snorted.

Roman sat forward on the couch, hands clasped, all humor gone from his face. "Which brings me to why I came today."

Lysander had an idea what Roman was going to say. "No."

Roman looked shocked. "No? I have not yet had a chance to tell you my thoughts."

"Still." Lysander shook his head. "No,"

Roman sighed. "Lysander, please. I only need a few moments of your time."

How was he supposed to resist sad vampire eyes? "Okay, but be warned. I've already spoken with my mother and come to an agreement with her."

"It is too late then." The sadness on Roman's face stabbed Lysander in the heart. "I thought I would give you some time for emotions to calm down from the excitement of our last meeting. I did not realize you would act so quickly."

"I'm sorry, Roman. I don't want to hurt you."

Roman tried to smile, but it faltered. His face settled into acceptance. "Since I am already here, how about I explain about a vampire's Bloodmate bond? That way if anything changes, you'll understand what a mating entails."

Roman got up and kneeled in front of Lysander's chair. Reaching up, he gently held Lysander's hands. "I understand you have a valid reason to reject our bonding, but I think you should know the price your decision could cost the both of us."

Lysander went to pull his hands away, then stopped. He nodded. "That's fair. If there's a price to pay, then I should know what it is."

"Thank you, Lysander. First, you need to understand that a Bloodmate bond is exceptionally rare. It happens so infrequently, most vampires believe the sacred bond to be nothing more than a myth. I, myself, know of only one other vampire who found his Bloodmate. And, as I said before, I have been searching for mine for almost a thousand years."

"Wow."

"Indeed." Roman settled back on his heels. "Second, those who find and bond with their fated mates are supposed to develop additional powers. This power exchange happens on both sides, which would mean I would gain some enhanced ability, but so would you."

"That doesn't make sense. I don't have any magic, so what could I possibly gain?"

"That I cannot tell you. I only know abilities are supposed to be gifted to both partners of the bonding couple. If this is true, it could possibly help your situation with your mother. Third, and probably most important, once a vampire has found and begun bonding with his fated Bloodmate, he will not be able to stand another's touch. He will also be unable to sustain himself from other blood sources. A broken bond will cause the vampire to eventually fade. That is, unless he goes feral from blood lust. Then he will need to be put down."

"Oh, shit," Lysander grabbed his hands and squeezed. "We haven't started to bond though, so you should be fine. Right? Roman, you're not saying anything. Tell me you haven't started bonding with me."

Roman looked at him, compassion and sadness in his face. "My understanding was that an exchange of blood was necessary to begin the bonding process. As it turns out, being in close proximity seems to have been enough in this case. It may have something to do with you coming from a magical bloodline."

Lysander jumped up, moving away. "Oh, no." He grabbed his hair with both hands. "What have I done?" He turned back. "You can stop this, can't you? You're super powerful, so you should be okay if we don't go near each other anymore, right? If we don't let it progress any further?"

Roman hesitated, looking at him, eyes heavy with pain and something Lysander couldn't quite read. Resignation perhaps? "Of course. I am old and powerful. I should be fine."

Lysander took a step closer, caught himself, then moved back. "Roman, this isn't what I want, but there are reasons I have to do this. Reasons that might save my brother, myself, and many others who depend on Bryan. If I was able to help and turned my back, I wouldn't be able to live with the guilt. But you shouldn't have to suffer either. Oh Goddess, I don't know the right thing to do." He pulled at his hair again and started pacing around the room.

"Lysander, hush. I do not want you to stress about this any further." Roman stood up. "A bond should be celebrated, not be the cause of such sadness and turmoil." He walked over and caressed Lysander's cheek. "I will respect your wishes and let you do what you must. Everything will sort itself out the way it was meant to be."

When Roman gently kissed his forehead, Lysander knew there was something he wasn't telling him. But it was too late to ask as he was already walking to the door. Roman stopped with his hand on the doorknob. "Take care of yourself, Lysander. Be happy."

With those parting words, he was gone.

That night, as Lysander was getting ready for bed, he felt a strong pull coming from outside. Looking out the window, he saw a shadow standing just outside the glow from the streetlight. It was Roman. He could feel his sadness across the distance. Lysander shook his head and spoke softly. "Please go home, Roman. Don't do this to yourself." He drew the shade and went to bed.

Any tears he shed that night were between him and Jinx

Sheri Eleese

Chapter Six

Edgar paced in front of Max's desk, waving his hands in agitation. "Max, you have to do something. It's been days and he just sits there, brooding and snarling at everyone. He won't handle coven issues, he's yelling at the staff, he won't sign the documents I give him, and now he's missing appointments, including the centennial meeting with Carlos to renew the treaty between our covens. Do you have any idea how long that took me to set up?"

Max's brow furrowed. "If we don't have that treaty in place, there will be no controlling Carlos. He'll use that as an excuse to try to take over our territory."

Edgar threw his hands in the air. "I know."

"Are you sure Roman missed that meeting?"

"Of course, I'm sure he missed the meeting. It's my job to know what Roman does. I schedule everything that happens in his life." Edgar kept pacing, growing more distressed. "The problem is, Roman's not doing anything. He won't listen to me and refuses to reschedule his appointments. I can't even get in to see him anymore since he's locked himself in his suite. You're his Second. I need you to try and get through to him."

"Of course. I didn't realize it had gotten so bad."

"That's not even the worst." Edgar leaned over the desk and whispered so none of the vampires outside of the office could hear. "I don't think he's eating either. I'm worried something is seriously wrong with him."

"Leave it with me, Edgar." Max stood up. "You get that meeting with Carlos rescheduled. I'll make sure Roman gets there."

"Thank you." Edgar hurried from the office.

"Roman, what the hell is going on with you?" Max muttered as he followed Edgar out the door, mentally preparing for what was sure to be a difficult discussion.

* * *

Roman was sprawled on his couch, arm slung over his face, his eyes sheltered in the crook of his elbow. His other arm dangled over the side; glass of whisky loosely held in his fingertips. He was doing his best to ignore the banging on his door, but Max was nothing if not persistent.

"Roman, answer this damn door before I break it down."

Hah. He'd like to see him try. His door was the best money could buy; custom made steel reinforced with magic, and secured by military grade locks. Nobody was getting through it. Not even Max.

Roman reached over with his free hand to the coffee table, patting around blindly until he found the remote. Once he located it, he turned up the music to drown out the racket Max was making.

It took him a few minutes to realize the banging had stopped. "Good," he muttered, taking a sip of his drink. He wasn't in the mood to talk to anyone.

Roman relaxed, sinking back into thoughts of his mate, imagining what it would have been like to spend his long life living and loving with his Zander. Ahh, Zander. That was his special name for his mate. Everyone called him something different, but Zander was for him alone. Roman took another sip of his drink, trying to think through his increasingly cloudy thoughts. When was the last time he ate? No matter, he'd just lay here and think about his precious mate. Hopefully Zander was doing okay. He sure missed him.

Roman really wished he could think of a way to have Zander before it was too late, but short of forcing the bond on him, he couldn't come up with a solution. And he would never do that. One did not intentionally harm their Bloodmate. Besides which, Zander would kick his ass if he tried. Thinking of his fierce mate doing so made Roman smile. Damn his almost mother-in-law for creating this situation anyway.

Wait a minute. Roman sat up abruptly, whisky sloshing in his glass. Wait just one damned minute. Instead of trying to change Zander's mind, he should be thinking of a way to get rid of his mother. If there was no mother, there would be no problem. And Zander would never have to know what he'd done. Roman tossed the rest of his drink back, looking at his empty glass. This was excellent whisky. It really helped with problem-solving.

Hearing a strange noise, Roman cocked his head, then turned to the door. It sounded like someone was using a blowtorch. Was someone trying to burn down his door? Roman sniffed. The scorching smell of molten metal filled the air, irritating his nasal passages. Someone really was trying to force their way in. But who in all the hells would be stupid enough to…Max! It had to be.

Roman was standing in the center of his entertainment area with his arms crossed when his super secure door was kicked in. Max stepped over the threshold. looking like some kind of action hero in a B grade flick. He was dressed all in black, blowtorch resting on his shoulder, smoke billowing around him as he strode into the room. He didn't even have a hair out of place.

"Something I can help you with?" Roman asked.

"Shut it." Max pointed the blowtorch at Roman. "What in the ever-loving hell do you think you're doing?"

"I was enjoying a lovely glass of whisky until someone burned down my door." Roman turned and made his way to his wet bar, grabbing a glass decanter. He held it up. "Can I get you a drink?"

"No, I don't want a bloody drink. I want to know why you blew off the meeting with Carlos. Are you trying to start a war?"

Roman took a sip from his freshly filled glass. "Hmm?"

"Are you even listening to me?"

"Of course. I don't have a meeting with Carlos."

Max growled in frustration. "Not now you don't." He threw down the blowtorch. Roman winced when it bounced off his hardwood floors, leaving scratches in the wood. "You were supposed to have a meeting with him last week, but you didn't show. Edgar has been trying to get you to reschedule but apparently you're not cooperating."

"Bah." Roman waved his hand dismissively. "Edgar's always going on about some meeting or other. I have more important things to worry about."

"In a minute you're going to be worrying about my foot in your ass. That's if I can fit it around your big fat head." Max stomped over him. "Edgar also says you're not eating. From how pale you are, I can see he's right about that too."

"It seems Edgar has a lot to say these days."

"That's not fair. He cares about you. As do I. Tell me what's going on. This behavior isn't like you."

Roman froze, staring into the bottom of his glass. Long minutes passed.

"Roman, I'm your friend as well as your Second. You can talk to me about anything. Please," Max gasped when Roman lifted his head, no longer able to hide the devastation he was feeling from his mate rejecting him. "What happened?"

Crossing the room, Roman dropped on the couch, holding his glass loosely between his parted legs. He sighed. "I told Lysander he was my Bloodmate."

"Congratulations. I'm so happy for you."

"Don't start celebrating yet." Roman raised his glass and took a healthy slug. "Zander is getting married on Saturday."

Max frowned. "You didn't tell me you were getting married?"

Roman snorted. "Because I'm not. My mate, however, is getting married."

"To who?"

Roman shrugged. "Some woman his mother picked out to."

"He can't do that. Roman, you have to stop him."

"I cannot. He has denied my claim."

"But you're Bloodmates. Why would he do that?"

"Why indeed?" Roman leaned back on the couch and closed his eyes. "His mother was forcing his brother into an undesirable marriage and Zander is taking his place."

"I still don't understand why."

"Apparently, his mother has been blackmailing Zander's brother, Bryan, his whole life by making threats against Zander if he doesn't do what she says. Since Zander doesn't have any power, he can't stop her." Roman's eyes popped open. "Though I have my doubts about that. Nonetheless, his mother's threats against him force his brother to toe the line. This time; however, Zander is determined to protect his brother by taking his place. He feels he owes it to Bryan."

"That sounds like a poorly written soap opera."

"I am aware. It is almost too tragic to be believable."

"It's a bloody mess, is what it is. But this changes nothing. You can't let him marry someone else. Maybe kidnap him or something. Whatever you have to do to stop this."

Roman glared at Max. "You think I have not thought about that? He would never forgive me." Roman shook his head. "No, I have to respect his wishes in this."

"Forever is a long time. He'd get over it."

"Perhaps, but it is not a chance I'm prepared to take. But all is not lost. I have just come up with a fool-proof plan."

"Oh?"

"Yes. If I make his mother disappear, all of our problems go with her." He saluted Max with his glass.

Max snorted. "That's your plan. To kill your mate's mother? That sounds like a good idea to you? Roman, do you really think your mate would ever forgive that?"

"Of course, he would. Especially since I have no intention of telling him."

"Roman, you might want to consider another…"

Boom!

A loud explosion rocked the building. Roman jumped up, staggering sideways when there was a second explosion. Max grabbed his arm, steadying him. A third explosion had them stumbling against each other as they started for the door. Screams could be heard coming from the floor below.

"Roman," Edgar yelled, appearing in the doorway. He leaned into the room, blood leaking from a shallow cut on his forehead. He startled, then looked at the scorch marks around the doorframe and the melted door lying on the ground. "What happened to your door?"

"Never mind that. What's going on?"

"It's Carlos. His vampires are attacking."

* * *

Fifteen minutes earlier…

Bryan dropped into Darkness Friday evening, hoping for a few minutes of relaxation after a stressful week. He was seated at his customary barstool, considering then discarding options as he tried to think of a way to stop his mother. Unfortunately, no matter how he twisted and turned his ideas, he couldn't come up with a palatable solution to prevent tomorrow's wedding.

"Is this seat taken?"

Bryan glanced over at the smaller vampire climbing onto the stool next to him. "Help yourself." He raised an eyebrow at the hand that was thrust in front of him.

"I'm Edgar."

"Hey, Edgar, I'm not interested." Bryan shifted away.

"No need to be a dick. I was just being friendly." Edgar turned to the bartender. "John, bring me a Cosmopolitan." He glared at Bryan's snort. "What's your problem?"

Snickering, Bryan said, "A Cosmopolitan? Really?"

"Shut up, neanderthal. Nobody asked you." Edgar turned to look at the people dancing, muttering under his breath. Bryan was pretty sure he heard big, dumb, ape.

Goddess, but he was being an ass. Bryan's shoulders slumped. "Sorry. It's been a stressful week. Doesn't excuse me from being a dick. Let's try this again." He held out his hand. "I'm Bryan. Pleased to meet you, Edgar. Can I buy you a drink?"

Edgar looked at his hand, seemingly deciding if he was worth the trouble. Finally shaking, he said, "No need. I'm Roman's Assistant. He doesn't charge his staff if we keep our tabs within reason."

"That's cool. I haven't seen Roman around the last few days. How's he doing."

A slow pan of eyes in his direction.

"How do you know Roman and why do you care?"

"Well, you see…" Bryan looked up at movement over Edgar's shoulder. "Get down." He dived forward, knocking Edgar to the floor and covering him with his body. Bryan wrapped his arms protectively over his head as explosions filled the room. Bottles shattered and plaster rained down from the ceiling. Screams pierced the air. Bryan conjured a protective shield above himself and Edgar, but didn't do it fast enough to prevent them from being covered with debris from the initial explosions. He pushed up on his hands, coughing as he tried to see through the smoke and dust that filled the air.

"Let me up. I have to check on Roman." Edgar knocked Bryan off of him, then scrambled up.

"Edgar, wait." Too late, he banged into Bryan's shield, bouncing back to land on his ass. He glared at Bryan, who winced, then thinned the shield so he could get through. A moment later Edgar was running up the stairs. Bryan expanded his shield to shelter the bartender and the few customers taking cover under the counter, stretching it from ceiling to floor. No sooner had he finished then something came flying across the room, slamming into it. Glowing red eyes and pointed teeth filled his vision. Vampire.

* * *

Roman jumped down the last few stairs, taking in the destruction of his club with a glance. Shattered glass, broken furniture, parts of the ceiling and walls were missing, broken bodies were lying on the floor. In the midst of the chaos, in the eye of the storm he'd created, surveying the destruction as his vampires laid waste to Roman's haven, was Carlos.

Roman sped across the room in a blinding rush of fury, slashing any vampire unfortunate enough to get in his way. Max followed behind, finishing off any vampire Roman left standing and protecting his back against new attacks. Roman caught a glimpse of Edgar and his bartender John helping some humans out the side door.

Knowing his assistant would get everyone to safety, Roman focused on reaching Carlos. He worked his way steadily across the dance floor—which was crawling with fighting vampires—stopping to help one of his bouncers who was outmatched three to one. They finished off the attackers in short order, then Roman kept going. Reaching his target, Roman rushed Carlos, driving him into the wall behind him. Carlos bounced back, flying into Roman and sending them both crashing to the floor. Claws flashed and fangs tore into any body part they could reach as hisses filled the air.

Carlos managed to get past Roman's guard, catching him on the shoulder with his razor-sharp teeth, tearing open a huge gash, parting Roman's flesh down to the bone.

Roman could feel himself weakening as blood poured from the wound. Knowing he needed to end the fight quickly, he ignored the damage Carlos was now inflicting along his side, focused on trying to rip his head off. But already weakened from lack of nourishment, Roman struggled to maintain the upper hand. His hands were slippery with blood as he gave a final effort to destroy his opponent.

Carlos, possibly seeing him falter, dug his claws in deep and yanked, tearing out a large chunk out of Roman's side.

Roman screamed as he pulled away, getting in a final slash across Carlos' cheek and across his throat. As Carlos dived at him, a body came flying across the room, knocking him to the side. Carlos slid across the floor, crashing to a stop when he hit the DJ's stage.

"Roman, are you okay? Shit. You're bleeding everywhere." Max's voice was frantic as he put pressure on Roman's wounds. "Why aren't you healing? Edgar, we need blood. Now." Max's voice was getting further away. "Roman. Don't you pass out on me. Roman. Edgar, hurry."

Roman succumbed to the dark.

Blood filled his mouth, pooling in his throat, choking him. Gagging, he coughed, spraying it everywhere.

"It's not working, he won't drink it. Roman, you have to swallow the blood or you won't heal"

"S'kay. Better this way," he slurred, sinking back into darkness.

"Roman!"

Chapter Seven

Bryan tapped softly on the doorframe, haggard after a long night dealing with the aftermath of the vampire attack. "Hello in here. I want to give someone an update. The bartender sent me up here."

"Sure. Come in," a vampire said.

Bryan stepped in the room. "I've finished with the authorities. They have everything they need and are leaving now. All the injured have been cared for and taken away."

"How many dead?"

Bryan grimaced. "Around twenty. The majority of those killed were vampires, most of them from the attackers. Unfortunately, there were also three humans killed."

"Damn it." The vampire rubbed his hand over his face. "And the bar?"

"I had the staff board up the holes as best they could. They're trying to clean up the mess now that the authorities have taken away the bodies and spoken to everyone. You don't have to worry. Everything that can be done right now is being looked after."

"Thanks. I really appreciate you taking care of that mess downstairs."

"No problem. I'm glad I was here to help." Bryan hesitated. "Sorry, I didn't get your name."

"I'm the one who's sorry. This night is making me forget my manners." The vampire held out his hand. "I'm Max, Roman's Second. And you're Lysander's brother, Bryan, right?"

"Yes." Bryan said slowly. "I don't recall meeting you before."

"We haven't been formally introduced, but I've seen you and your brother in the bar. Plus, Roman has talked about you both."

Bryan shook his hand. "I see. It's good to meet you Max. I wish it was under better circumstances." Bryan frowned when Max continued holding his hand.

"Sorry." Max let go of him, his fingertips lingering before dropping away.

Bryan's eyes narrowed, wondering at the tingle left in the wake of Max's touch. Then a possible reason came to him. He quickly locked down his personal shields, feeling them slam them into place with unusual firmness.

Max frowned at his fingers, then looked at Bryan, then back to his hand.

When Max's attention came back to him, Bryan forced a calm he didn't feel, raising his eyebrow in question. Max finally turned away with a puzzled look on his face. Bryan breathed a quiet sigh of relief, hoping that hadn't been what he thought it was. And that he'd got his shields in place in time if it was. He really didn't have room in his life for that kind of complication.

Following Max over to Roman's side, Bryan tipped his chin. "How's he doing?"

Edgar looked up, his eyes red-streaked and watery. He was brushing Roman's hair back from his forehead. "It's not good. He's not healing and won't drink any blood. I just don't understand why."

Bryan's concerned look turned to dismay. "Is this because of his bond with my brother?"

"Bond? Brother?" Edgar looked bewildered. "What bond?"

Max interrupted. "Sorry, Bryan, this is Edgar, Roman's Assistant."

"Yes, we met downstairs before the attack." Bryan nodded to Edgar.

"Never mind that. What bond are you talking about?" Edgar's face was starting to look panicked.

"Roman and I were talking just before the attack. Lysander, Bryan's brother, is Roman's Bloodmate. He rejected Roman's bond. That's why Roman hasn't been himself lately."

"Rejected his bond," Edgar shrieked. "He can't do that." He rushed over to Bryan, grabbing the front of his shirt and shaking him. "You have to find him and bring him here. Immediately. Roman will die if he doesn't get blood right away. And your brother is the only one he can drink from." Edgar pushed him back. "Why are you still standing here? Go!"

* * *

Lysander paced from one end of his mother's study to the other, nervously tugging on his sleeves. He reached up for the thousandth time to pull at the collar of his shirt. His tie was too tight, choking him the longer he wore it. His stomach had been in turmoil all morning and he had a burning pain in his side and neck that he couldn't explain.

Lysander pivoted when he reached the wall, then came to an abrupt stop. "Mother."

Charlotte glided into the room, pale blonde hair in a fancy updo, resplendent in a navy chiffon dress. "Have you heard from Bryan?"

"No. He's not answering his phone."

"There's no sense waiting for him any longer. Everyone of importance is here, so we may as well get started." Charlotte looked him over, her mouth pursing, apparently finding him lacking in some manner. "Clean yourself up. I don't want any of my guests seeing you looking so disheveled. I'll have them hold the proceedings for ten minutes. Be on time and be presentable. Do you understand?"

"Yes, Mother. Just as I understand that once I go through with this, you'll leave Bryan alone."

Charlotte laughed, shaking her head. "Leave Bryan alone? I hardly think so. With you married to Jillian, I'll have my alliance with the Frone clan." Charlotte tsked at him, shaking her head. "You're a fool if you think I wouldn't find a strategic match for your brother as well. I've already made arrangements for an alliance with the Cabot clan, which will be secured once Bryan marries whichever daughter they've selected. In a couple more months, I'll finally be positioned to challenge the Council."

Damn it. He knew it. He wished he could say he was surprised, but he really wasn't. Hiding his dismay, Lysander acted out his part in the charade he was playing. "No. You can't do that." Clenching his fists, he came to a halt in front of Charlotte. "We had a deal, Mother."

"Now I have another deal." Charlotte glanced at her watch, ignoring his anger. "You better hurry along. You only have eight minutes left."

"You were supposed to let both of us go. You promised."

"Stop with the dramatics. I promised nothing. I was never going to let you go. As long as I control you, I control your brother." With a regal tilt to her head, Charlotte headed out of the room. "Seven minutes. Don't be late."

Lysander was distressed by this latest betrayal, even knowing beforehand that it was coming. Hardening his heart, he ruthlessly severed his final hope of his mother ever putting her sons before her ambitions. He was done with her. Done with her scheming and done with her maneuvering to control the Council. From now on he was going to do everything he could to help Bryan stop her.

First; however, he needed to escape this farce of a marriage, then he would find Roman. And he had to get moving fast. There were only a few minutes left before his mother would come looking for him.

At that moment, Bryan rushed in through the French doors that led off from the garden. "Thank the Goddess you're still here. Hurry, come with me." He grabbed a handful of Lysander's suit jacket, pulling him toward the door. "We have no time to waste if we're going to save him."

"Save who?"

"Roman. He's been badly hurt and needs you."

Lysander froze, forcing Bryan to stop. "Roman's hurt?"

"Yes, come on. We need to hurry." Bryan got him moving again.

The drapes were still swaying in the breeze coming through the open French doors when the office door slammed open with a loud bang.

"Time's up. Everyone is waiting."

It took seconds for Charlotte to realize the office was empty. Her teeth clenched in rage and she could feel circles of heat on her checks. "You will regret this, child. You will pay. Your brother will pay." With a final sweeping glance of the room, Charlotte forced herself to calm, then called out to her companion waiting in the hallway.

"Jillian, dear, it seems we have a problem."

* * *

Lysander rushed past Bryan, racing into the room. He came to a stop when he took in the horrifying sight of Roman in his bed, lying still as death. With some young guy stroking his hair. He choked down a snarl seeing his mate being touched by someone else. Startled eyes snapped in his direction. Perhaps he didn't choke that back as much as he thought.

Hurrying to get to Roman's side, he crashed into a body that appeared out of nowhere. Hands grabbed his arms to steady him, but didn't let him go. Bryan came and stood beside him. "It's okay, Max. It's only Lysander."

Max looked Lysander over, clearly unimpressed by whatever he saw. There was a lot of that going around today. "I am fully aware of who this is." A tic showed in Max's jaw when his teeth clenched. "It's because of him Roman's in this state. Why are you even here?"

"I'm here to help Roman if I can."

"Again, I ask, why?"

Lysander was perplexed. "Because Bryan said he's dying. I have to try to save him. Bryan said my blood could help him."

"You rejected him. Why does it matter?"

Lysander was starting to get angry at this guy blocking his way. He didn't have time for all these questions. "It's none of your business. I don't owe you any explanations. Now move out of my way." He tried pushing Max's chest, but the asshole wouldn't budge.

"Let me repeat myself because it seems you're not understand. Why are you bothering to save him? Is it your intention to complete your bond?"

"I don't know, maybe?"

Max shoved him away and crossed his arms. "If you're not going to finish bonding with him, it's best that you go now. Roman needs to be surrounded by those who love him when he dies. I'm for damn sure not going to let you save him, only for him to suffer and die in the next few days when you don't bond with him."

"Die?" Lysander's eyes widened. "Nobody's going to die. I'm here to save him, which I can't do unless you get the hell out of my way." Lysander pushed against Max again, who still wouldn't move. "Let me through, asshole."

"Max," Bryan interrupted. "Ease up a moment, I think we're missing some information. Why is Roman going to die?"

Max sneered at Lysander. "If your pathetic brother doesn't finish the bond with Roman, he will fade and die. Right now, it will happen quickly because he's gravely injured and lost too much blood. But either way, he will die because the bond is incomplete. It would be more humane to let him go now than draw this out and make him suffer needlessly."

"No." Lysander finally pushed around Max, rushing to Roman's side. "He said everything would be fine. That he could stop the process. He would have told me if he was in danger."

"Would he? Or would he have wanted to spare his mate being forced to choose between his brother and him?"

Lysander dropped to his knees, grabbing Roman's hand. "I'm sorry. Oh, Roman, I'm so sorry. I made such a mistake. Please, you have to fight and get better. Please." He raised his head to the guy still stroking Roman's hair, who had better stop right freaking now. "Who are you?"

The touchy-feely guy glared at Lysander. "Edgar." He turned back to Roman. "Now, are you going to save him or not? If not, there's the door." His shaking finger pointed imperiously to the entrance, before he began stroking Roman's hair again. Seriously, he was going to lose that hand if he didn't stop touching Lysander's vampire.

"I'm not going anywhere. Tell me what I need to do." Lysander held still under Edgar's intense scrutiny, impatient as the pool of blood around Roman's body continued to grow.

Finally, Edgar nodded, standing up. "If he's to have any chance, he needs your blood. It will be easier to control him if you use your wrist. Pool as much blood in his mouth as you can and try to get him to swallow. His instincts should take over after that." Edgar looked at Roman, and gently stroked his hair, hand traveling down his cheek and finally resting over his heart. "If he accepts your blood, he should be fine in a day or two."

Speaking through gritted teeth, Lysander got right up in Edgar's face. "I'll give him my blood and heal him. As for right now, I suggest you take your hands off of him. When he's healed, you can explain who you are and why you keep touching my mate."

"Ooh, the kitten has claws. Why do you care? You didn't even want him."

"Edgar," Max warned.

"No, Max. Roman's in this condition because this idiot turned him away."

Lysander glared at Edgar. "I made the wrong choice. I had my reasons, but I was wrong. Do not make the mistake of thinking I'm too weak to fight for what is mine." He turned to Roman. "Once he's back on his feet, we'll settle this and see what place you'll have in his life. If any."

Edgar lunged for him, being pulled back when Max's hand shot out and grabbed him. "Now is not the time for this. Let Lysander heal him then you guys can fight it out. Here." Max handed Lysander a pocket knife, "You might find this easier than trying to rip open a vein; you don't have the teeth for it." Fangs flashed as Max hissed at him.

Awesome, no hostility here. Nope, none at all.

Lysander sat in the chair by the bed, not hearing when everyone left the room, his entire focus on his dying mate. His hands were shaking as he opened the knife. Blowing out a breath, he placed the sharpened edge against his wrist and sliced quickly.

He groaned when hot blood poured into his mouth, recognizing the scent. But no, he mustn't drink it. He'd promised. He tried moving his head but something was holding him. He had to get away.

"Roman, stop moving. It's okay. I need you to swallow."

He struggled to get words out, but he was so weak, "No. Not allowed."

"You have to swallow, Roman. Please. Do it for me."

"Can't. Bond. Let me die."

"Dear Goddess, what have I done to you?"

He knew that voice. But from where?

"Roman, I promise it will be okay. Everything will be fine as long as you swallow. Please, you must drink."

No. He tried pulling his head away again, still unable to break free.

A voice whispered in his ear, soothing him in the darkness. "Roman, it's Lysander. I need you to stop fighting me. Shhh. You must listen to me. This is very important. Roman, I freely accept your bond as your Bloodmate. Please, my mate, drink now, so you can heal."

His Bloodmate? He sounded worried. He should be happy. He would listen and do what he asked.

An arm pressed against his mouth, warm blood dripping. Grabbing hold with both hands, Roman drank.

Lysander, feeling weaker, his skin paler than when he arrived, joined the group waiting anxiously in Roman's living area. He sank down on the couch, hands over his face.

"What happened? What did you do to him now?" Edgar's frantic voice cut through the turmoil in his mind.

Lysander raised his head, emotion clogging his voice. "He's going to be fine. He's healing now."

"Praise the Goddess." Edgar sat down beside him. "Why are you so upset?"

"It was so close. He wouldn't take my blood. He kept fighting me, saying he couldn't bond. He could have died and it would've been my fault. I did that to him. Me. I'm responsible for making him so weak."

Slap. Lysander put his hand on his face and stared wide-eyed at Edgar.

"Snap out of it. We don't have time for your dramatics." Edgar stood. "I'm going to check on Roman to make sure he's fine and that you didn't mess this up. You pull yourself together. Roman will need a strong mate when he's better, not some wailing damsel in distress."

Edgar stomped off to Roman's room.

"He's right, Sandi. There's no sense beating yourself up for this. You had reasons for the decision you made, even though you were wrong. Get over it and move on, or you do both Roman and yourself a disservice." Typical Bryan, always logical and not afraid to bring the tough love.

Lysander nodded. "You're absolutely right. I promised Roman I'd complete the bond once he was healed. I'm not sure if he fully understood, but I will follow through." He stood up, swaying. "Whoa."

Bryan grabbed for him. "Are you all right?"

"Yes. I was just dizzy there for a moment. It seems better now." Lysander felt strangely unsettled, but passed it off as a side-effect of giving so much blood. "Can you stay here and keep an eye on Roman? I need to run home to pack a few things and grab Jinx if I'm going to be staying here."

"What, pray tell, is a Jinx?" Apparently, Max still had a stick up his butt. Lysander ignored him.

Bryan looked at him closely. "Are you sure you're okay? You seem a bit shaky."

"I'll be fine." Lysander headed for the door. "Thanks for staying with Roman, I shouldn't be too long."

"Seriously, what is a Jinx?" Bryan just laughed, before turning to explain to Max.

Lysander left him to it. He had more important things to focus on, like getting back to his mate as quickly as possible. He added sorting out what to do with Edgar to his list. Edgar, who was alone with his mate again. He'd better be keeping his hands to himself this time.

Sheri Eleese

Chapter Eight

Captured…

He hurt so bad. Lysander groaned when he tried moving and pain radiated throughout his entire body. He reached for his neck where the pain was the worst, but his arm wouldn't move. He looked to see why, but it was too dark. Panic started rising, then he realized his eyes were closed. He went to open them but something sticky coated his lashes, gluing them shut. He strained against the substance holding them closed. After lots of stretching and pulling of his eyelids—and tearing out some lashes—he was finally able to work them open.

Looking through bleary eyes, he saw his arms were stretched above his head, with his wrists in metal cuffs. A heavy chain was threaded through the cuffs and attached to a rusted ring in the ceiling. His toes barely touched the ground; his weight dangling from his cuffed wrists. He reached down with his toes, trying to relieve the pressure on his hands and screamed, nearly passing out when agony flared in his ankle, which felt like it was broken. He let his weight drop again, trying to ignore the burning in his wrists.

Peering around the room, he could see streaks of blood splattered on the stone walls and what looked like scattered bones and piles of rusty looking rags on the dirt floor. He suddenly realized he was naked. Looking down his body, he saw blood oozing down his chest from multiple spots. He squinted. Were those bite marks? It was hard to tell, but it looked as if a wild animal had been chewing on him.

How did he get here? The last thing he remembered was leaving Darkness to go pick up his cat.

"Someone's awake, I see." Lysander looked over to the vampire standing in the doorway. He was beautiful, but something in his cold, cruel eyes had him whimpering in terror. "I'm so glad you finally decided to join us. It's much more fun to feed when one can hear the screams." The vampire sauntered into the room, his blood-stained teeth almost glowing as they were hit by a stray beam of light coming through the narrow window high in the wall. His long, curly blond hair was strangely clumped and streaked with red. Reaching Lysander, he swiped a finger through a trail of tacky blood seeping down his chest. Raising it to his mouth, he sucked it off. "Delicious," he purred. "I'm going to have so much fun with you." He leaned in and extended his tongue, licking from Lysander's naval to his aching neck, where he sucked hard. Lysander started shaking, terrified when the vampire whispered in his ear. "You smell like him. It's barely there, but I can smell that bastard on you." He stepped back, his red-tinted eyes filled with madness. "Let's begin, shall we?" Grinning maniacally, he bared his razor-sharp teeth.

Red filled Lysander's vision. He started screaming.

* * *

Meeting the Elders in the Council Chambers…

Charlotte tilted her head regally, managing to look down her nose at the five Elders, despite the fact they sat at a dais above her. Elders Thomas, Ruth, Zachary, Olivia, and Peter, were relics from a time long gone who had outlived their relevance. They just didn't hadn't realized it yet. They had no idea how to get along in the current century, clinging to their moldered and outdated ideals, close-minded to any suggestion of progress. The very fact she had to bow down to their dictates was repugnant. They would rue the day they overruled her inclusion on the Council. They wouldn't understand their danger, wouldn't see her coming, until it was too late. Then she would eliminate them.

It was now time to set her final pieces in motion. Then they would learn who really had the power. But first, the game must be played.

"Esteemed Elders." Charlotte curtsied, grinding her teeth. "Thank you for granting my request for an audience."

"You may rise, child." A palsied hand motioned her forward. "What do you seek from this Esteemed and Erudite Council?"

Charlotte moved forward, locking down her distaste at having to participate in this pretentious sham of a proceeding. "If it may please Your Council, I implore upon you to order my oldest child, Bryan, to fulfill the Marriage Covenant between Clan Galway and Clan Cabot."

"Why would We deign to meddle in a personal domestic arrangement? This request is beneath Us."

She was going to crack a tooth if this went on too long. Goddess give her the strength not to throttle these decrepit fools until they drowned in their own drool. "If I may have your indulgence for a brief moment?" Charlotte waited for their approval before continuing. "Esteemed Council, though it pains me to admit, my oldest son is being recalcitrant in adhering to the arrangement that will unify our two clans. The Covenant was agreed to in the hope that bonding our clans would strengthen our bloodlines. Bloodlines that grow ever weaker every generation, sullied as they are by dalliances with humans. We must work to purify the bloodlines and restore the magic user community to the highest level of the paranormal hierarchy, as is our right." Charlotte took a step back and lowered her head, waiting upon their decision.

After some deliberation, Elder Thomas, with a great deal of effort, shakily stood and addressed her. "We find merit in your words. We will let Our wishes be known to Bryan Galway, that he is ordered to fulfill the terms of the Covenant with Clan Cabot. Such matter to be completed within ten days. Thus is Our will."

"Goddess' Blessings upon you, Esteemed Elders." Charlotte's curtsey hid her triumphant grin. Stupid, pathetic fools.

* * *

Roman bolted upright, screaming and grabbing at his chest, "Lysander."

"What? What's wrong?" Max and Edgar rush into the room.

"Something's wrong with Lysander." Roman attempted to get out of bed, but the blankets were tangled around his legs, stopping him. He tried to shake them free. Hands were then pushing him back down. He slapped at them, baring his fangs. "Move out of my way. I need to get to Zander."

"Roman," Max's voice thundered. "You almost died and haven't finished healing. Lie the hell down."

"No, I have to go. Lysander needs me."

"You should be worried about yourself, not Lysander. He's fine. You're the one who was mortally wounded."

Roman's eyes turned red as fury consumed him. He flew from the bed, crashing into Max, knocking them both to the floor. He hissed in Max's face from his perch on his chest. "Do not come between me and my Bonded." Hands pulled fruitlessly at his wrists, which were now wrapped around Max's neck. Nobody had the right to stop him from getting to his Bonded, not even Max. Roman pressed down harder, squeezing tightly. He barely felt the pain from Max's punches to his sides.

Edgar's voice finally broke through his rage, screaming hysterically. "Roman, stop. Max, stop fighting. Both of you, stop it now!"

A pitcher of water was dumped over Roman's head.

Shocked out of his rage, Roman stared into Max's frightened eyes. What was he doing? Had he lost his mind? Max was his most trusted friend, his right-hand man. Roman hurriedly stood, offering Max a hand up. "I'm sorry, Max. I don't know what came over me."

"You thought I'd threatened your Bonded, though I don't know why. Lysander's grabbing a few things from home. He should be back shortly."

Roman shook his head, rubbing his chest. "No. Something's wrong. I think Zander is in trouble."

Edgar spoke up. "How can you tell? You haven't even fully bonded yet. Maybe it was something you ate."

Roman narrowed his eyes, glaring at Edgar. "Is there a problem here?"

Edgar crossed his arms, nose in the air. "He refused you and showed you no respect. He's no better than a magicless human and not good enough to be your Bonded. You deserve better."

"You dare malign my Bonded? My fated mate?" Roman roared, towering over Edgar, who shrank back. He stalked him, hissing and growling, as Edgar edged backward. "I am your Prince and control whether you live or die. Get out of my sight before I tear your head off."

Whimpering, Edgar edged around Roman, keeping his back to the wall and leaving as much space between them as possible. The moment the way was clear, he fled through the newly replaced door, slamming it behind him.

"Prince Roman?" Max questioned.

"Not now, Max." Roman's fangs gnashed as he paced, furious. How dare they question his mate?

"Umm, Roman, don't you think you might be overreacting?"

Roman spun around, crowding Max to the wall, and hissed in his face.

"This," Max waved his hand. "This is what I'm talking about. This is not normal. What's the matter with you?"

Frowning, Roman pulled back, having to exert much more effort than should have been necessary to bring himself under control. "I don't know. I think it has to do with Zander. Something is wrong."

"I told you, he's fine. He just ran home to pick up his cat."

"His cat? Jinx?" Roman grimaced. "A cat in the coven? Oh no, there will be no cat, not even Jinx."

"Oh yes, definitely a cat." Laughter erupted from Max, breaking the tension. "It comes with your Bonded. You don't have a choice." Roman's scowl made Max laugh harder.

Rapid banging on the door interrupted them. "Max, are you in there? Max." Max opened the door, catching Bryan as he fell through. Bryan grabbed his shirt with his fists, frantically pulling. "You have to help me. Lysander is missing." Max's head swiveled to Roman.

"I knew something was wrong with Zander." Roman yanked Bryan away from Max. "Tell me what you know."

"I don't know anything. He just vanished. He never made it home when he left here. I can't reach his phone. I've tried scrying and I still can't find any sign of him."

Roman turned to Max. "Go check the security feeds. Have Edgar question the coven. Somebody must have seen something." As Max rushed through the door, he pointed to Bryan. "You stay here and keep trying to reach him."

Roman grimaced, rubbing his chest again. His anxiety suddenly increased. He knew, without a moment's doubt, that they needed to find Lysander now or it would be too late.

Bryan stepped in front of him. "You have a link with my brother, don't you? Can't you figure out where he is?"

Roman paused. The bond was incomplete, but perhaps? Realizing he was still worrying at his chest, he focused on the feeling, startled when he realized it wasn't coming from him. It was Zander.

He sank deep into his core, frantically trying to find the path. There, a barely realized connection, a thin strand pulsing softly, growing fainter even as he stretched his awareness. Desperately, he fed power down the link, trying to keep Lysander alive until they could find him.

Max rushed into the room. "The camera's show him being grabbed off the street. It was Carlos. Carlos took Lysander."

Roman roared in fury, his fangs elongating and his turning eyes fiery red. "He will die for touching what is mine."

* * *

Lysander stirred; his thoughts hazy "Roman?"

Struggling to see through blood encrusted, swollen eyes, he had shadowy impressions of movement, but no Roman. Strange. It felt like Roman was with him. His head wobbled on his shoulders; body still hanging from cuffs and chains. He couldn't feel his arms anymore, which was a relief. The rest of his body was a giant, festering, agony filled wound. He closed his eyes, sinking back into darkness where pain was a distant memory. Maybe Roman was in the darkness waiting for him.

Lysander floated back to the surface when tremors shook the building, rattling the chains keeping him suspended. Fragments shook loose from the ceiling, creating small clouds of dust when they hit the ground. Rust particles, breaking free from his restraints, rained down on him. Coughing weakly through the dusk and the smoke, Lysander ears rang as shouts and screams filled the air. Something that made a horrible growling noise was closing in on him. Lysander began shaking What new hells were they going to torture him with now? Head lolling, he closed his eyes, not wanting to see what shape death wore.

"He's in here."

"Dear Goddess. What did they do to him?"

"Someone hold Roman back. Max, get Sandi down from there before Roman breaks free. Roman, stop. You need to calm down. You're going to hurt your mate."

"I've got him."

Lysander felt himself floating, sinking down until he landed somewhere that felt warm and safe. He sighed. This was a good place to die.

"Roman, control yourself. I'm not going to hurt him. I'm just trying to see. Damn it. That hurt."

"Max. Go after Carlos. He's getting away."

"Never mind him. We need to get Roman and Lysander out of here."

Someone sniffed, "Sandi, I'm so sorry I failed you. You need to hold on. We're taking you home."

Bryan? Was he still dreaming? But there was a voice missing. Where was it? He shifted restlessly, searching. Whimpers filled the air. Someone was hurt. Who?

"My sweet, precious mate. You must stop moving before you injure yourself further. Hush, sweetness, I've got you now. I'll keep you safe."

He stilled, listening to the soothing voice which flowed over him like warm rain on a sunny day. He breathed deep through his broken, crushed nose; the smell of leather and musk reassuring. He whimpered as he turned into the warmth, taking it with him as he let himself drift, the darkness pulling him under once more.

The next time awareness came, his body was on fire. Screaming, he curled away from the teeth coming for him in the dark. Tortured cries filled the air. Hands kept pulling him back. Frantic, he fought harder to get away before they could hurt him again. Pain, oh, Goddess, so much pain.

"I can't heal him. He's fighting it off somehow."

"I've got him." Such a wonderful, powerful voice. He stopped moving, not wanting to miss any words. "Everyone out now."

"But Roman…"

"Get out. I will look after my mate." Gentle hands stroked soothingly, cooling his burning skin. "Zander, listen to me. Do you understand me?" Head lolling to the voice, he gave a small bob. "Good, you're doing great."

He felt himself floating like a balloon. He was flying. Maybe he could touch the sky? Oh, the darkness; falling, he was falling, sinking into gray.

"Zander, come back to me. Focus on my voice. Dear Goddess, please help me. I'm losing him." The wonderful voice; so sad. He struggled through clouds of black, straining to find it, lost in the shadows. "Zander, listen to my voice. I must give you my blood. It's the only thing that can save you now. It will lock the bond, give you something to hold onto. Do you understand?"

He started drifting on the waves of air, floating, soaring in the wind.

"Lysander." The voice was back, angry now. "There's no going back from this. Please Zander, I need you to freely accept the bond." Fading again. "Damn it, Lysander."

Warmth, like liquid sunshine, filled his mouth. Choking as he tried to breath it in, it went spraying, like butterflies drifting in the breeze. More filled his mouth, too much. His throat worked as it remembered how to swallow. Heat burning down his body, liquid rays of light rushing through him, his hands and feet on fire. More. So good. Heating him up. He'd been so cold. Glutting on the hot liquid pouring in, he swallowed. Warmth spilled out the sides of his mouth.

"That's good, Zander. Enough. You're going to be fine. Rest now."

As he chased butterflies in his mind, words followed him on the wind.

"Goddess forgive me for what I have done."

Sheri Eleese

Chapter Nine

Lysander woke and pushed his cat's butt from his face, then spit out a piece of fur. He stretched fully, feeling the pull in all his muscles that you only got after a long, deep rest. Man, did he feel fantastic. That had to have been the best sleep he'd had in ages. Rolling to his side, his body slid against smooth, cool sheets. He stilled. This wasn't his bed.

Opening his eyes, he realized he wasn't in his bedroom. And wherever he was, it was large enough in here to fit his whole apartment. Sitting up, he looked around the room, searching for signs of who it belonged to, all the while, in the back of his mind, he was trying to figure out how he got here. Unfortunately, there was a distinct lack of personality in the stark and masculine room, making it hard to determine where he was.

Swinging his legs over the side of the bed, Lysander stood and stretched again, breathing deep. It was amazing how awesome he felt. Warning bells went off in his mind. Something was wrong with that thought. Then it came to him. He'd been hurt. Badly hurt.

Lysander started frantically patting over his body, searching for wounds that should be there. Since he was dressed only in sleep pants, it was easy to see there wasn't a mark on him. Which couldn't be right. He distinctly remembered being tortured. Surely that hadn't all been a dream? Morpheus wouldn't be so cruel.

Tiptoeing across the room, Lysander pressed his ear against a heavy oak door. Hearing nothing, he opened it a crack, peeking through, then exited into a long hallway, his footsteps muffled by the thick pile carpet. Stealthily making his way down the hallway, Lysander slowed when he came to an open doorway. Peering through, he was startled to find Roman sitting on a couch, hunched over with his face in his hands. Dejection was in every line of his body.

Roman's head snapped up when Lysander moved closer, relief and sorrow in his eyes. Lysander quickly closed the distance, sitting beside him and touching his arm. "What's wrong?"

"What's wrong? How can you even ask that?" Roman leaned away, then stood. Fists squeezing tight, he faced Lysander. "I betrayed you. How can you even stand to be near me?"

Lysander was puzzled. "What are you talking about?"

"I forced the bond on you, when I said I wouldn't. I swore I wouldn't, then when the first opportunity came along, I did it anyway. And I'm happy I did it, because it was the only way to save you. But now I've ruined everything. You'll never trust me again."

Lysander burst into laughter; which was the last thing Roman expected, judging by the shock on his face. It quickly changed to hurt. Motioning with his hands, Lysander said, "I'm sorry. It's just, you sounded so dramatic. How long have you been beating yourself up about this?"

Yes, disgruntled was a much better look than guilty or hurt. Roman reminded him of Jinx when he snatched away his favorite toy.

Lysander stood and placed his hands on Roman's cheeks. "You did nothing wrong. I already promised to bond with you, don't you remember?" Confusion gave way to relief, which was much better.

"Thank the Goddess. I was afraid you would hate me." Strong arms wrapped tightly around him. He settled easily into Roman's hold.

Peering up, Lysander decided to tease his vampire, "Since we're bonded now and we didn't even get to do it the fun way, don't you think it's time you kissed me?"

"You make a valid point. That is an oversight I will immediately correct." Roman's hands covered his cheeks as he leaned in, pausing so they could share breaths, before he pressed their lips together.

Lysander breathed him in, pulling his musky scent deep into his lungs.

Roman's lips moved slowly over his, pressing, adjusting, tongue teasing, sipping softly. Warmth and joy flooded his senses. The kiss deepened. Slow, drugging kisses quickly escalated, turning frantic with hunger and need. Lysander's gasp allowed Roman to breach his parted lips. He delved deep, tasting, plundering.

Deep in his core, something stirred. Akin to a baby bird waking up, preparing to stretch his wings; a seed, sending out shoots, petals unfurling, ready to face the sun. Then it settled back into its peaceful state, not yet ready to emerge, but still pulsing with a subdued glow.

Later, Lysander would wonder what that was. At the moment, his vampire had his full attention.

Roman pulled back, his breaths stirring Lysander's hair. "Please, Zander, let me have you and complete the bond." He dove into his mouth again, not waiting on a response.

Lysander broke free long moments later, taking a much-needed breath. Resting his forehead on Roman's, he gasped, "I thought we were already bonded."

Softly kissing his nose, Roman whispered, "There is one step left to make the bond so strong it will survive anything, even death. It requires an exchange of sex and blood."

Lysander chuckled. "I bet you say that to all the boys."

Roman kissed him firmly in retaliation. As a punishment, it wasn't very effective.

Coming up for air again, Lysander asked, "Are you sure you want to be tied more firmly to me? I don't have much to offer other than a psychotic mother and an over-protective big brother. I have no magic and no standing in the magic user community. As a vampire leader, you deserve so much better in a mate."

Strong arms squeezed him gently. "Zander, you are perfect for me. You are strong, feisty, stubborn, and have a giving heart that cares deeply for others. I would be honored to be True-bonded to you, my precious Bloodmate." Another soft kiss. "Besides, you forgot to mention you also come with a cat." Roman shuddered.

Lysander laughed, grabbing his hand and leading him back to the bedroom. That was good enough for him. He'd been wanting a taste of Roman since the first time he'd seen him, before he knew what he was really like. And what he'd learned since then made Lysander want Roman even more.

And taking into consideration the drama of the last few days, they really needed to complete their bond before something else interrupted them.

Forbidden Bonds

* * *

Back at the Council Chambers…

Bryan stood before the Council with his arms crossed, unimpressed with being summarily summoned. He glared at Elder Thomas, who could barely sit upright, his great age finally catching up with him and surpassing the limits of what even magic could delay. Elders Ruth, Zachary, Olivia, and Peter, while still ancient, had energy comparable to middle-aged humans, sustained by their great powers.

Charlotte hissed from beside him, jabbing her elbow into his side. "Show respect for your betters." He gave her a long look, then edged sideways, beyond her elbow's reach.

Addressing the Council, Bryan asked, "Why have I been summoned?"

Elder Thomas' eyebrow raised. "You would speak to Us in that manner? Do you forget your place?"

"I'm quite aware of my place. I'm thinking it's you who have forgotten yours. In case it has slipped your mind, the Galway clan is the ruling faction among magic users. My father led your Council before his untimely death and I will be taking his place upon my thirtieth birthday."

"That is not yet decided. Your acceptance must still be voted and agreed on."

Bryan bit his tongue. He was about to greatly disrupt the proceedings but needed to bide his time until he found out why the Council—or his mother—had had him brought here. It would behoove him to determine their agenda before he hijacked the meeting. He needed to know who his enemies were, though he suspected it was all of them.

"My apologies." Bryan tipped his head. That was as much of a concession to politeness as he could manage.

Elder Thomas, perhaps realizing that was the best they could expect, got right to the point. "It has been brought to Our attention that a fortuitous match has been arranged between yourself and Clan Cabot. This match is of utmost importance to the future of magic users, as it will help facilitate the strengthening of the bloodlines of the clans. Bloodlines that are getting weaker with every generation due to interactions with humans. You have a duty to your clan, and the magic user community as a whole, to do your part in strengthening them. We, the Council, expect your obedience in this matter and are prepared to enforce compliance to it."

Bryan's head had slowly turned to his mother during Elder Thomas' speech, knowing who was to blame for this. Charlotte was almost quivering in her excitement. Feeling his death-glare, she looked at him and smiled victoriously, not daunted in the least. Damn her. He wasn't ready to take on the Council…or his mother and her accumulated allies. But because of this preposterous ploy, he was now out of time. Damn her twice for forcing his hand

Bryan turned back to Elder Thomas. "I regret to inform you that there will be no fortuitous match, regardless of my mother's maneuverings. The day the Council starts taking direction from an embittered, conniving, self-serving witch, is the day that proves you have outlived your usefulness. Your sense of importance has blinded you. Your lack of leadership and integrity demonstrates the need to have you replaced. It is past time for this relic of a Council to be dismantled so a new, inclusive Council can be put in place. A Council that will give fair guidance and leadership to all paranormal groups, not one that serves only themselves. The seats you hold are a privilege that come with the responsibility of governing fairly. You've tarnished those seats by using your positions and authority to reward those who pander to you and by threatening those who don't fall in line with your wishes."

Elder Ruth stood. "You dare to stand before this Esteemed Council and pass judgment?" She raised her hand, gathering power. Bryan stood unconcerned; his protection spell, which he'd prepared during his speech, was ready to be released.

Charlotte moved to stand near Ruth, also raising her hand to bring forth her power.

"You too, Mother? Has your ambition for power completely eroded your sense of morality and honor?" Bryan glared at her, his eyes promising revenge as he fed more power into his spell, preparing for the upcoming battle.

Power levels in the chamber rose. Bryan braced himself, his teeth clenched against the increased magic zinging through his nerve endings. He released the hold on his protection shield, snapping it into place mere seconds before the chamber was rocked by an outside force of earth-shattering power. The Council members and Charlotte, caught off guard by the fierce explosion, were knocked from their feet and sent tumbling across the floor.

Bryan, safe behind his shield, stared in amazement as power ripped through the room, tearing tapestries off walls, knocking over chairs, and preventing anyone from gaining their feet. His eyebrows shot up when the water pitcher from the council table flew across the room and shattered against the wall, soaking Charlotte and covering her with glass fragments.

When the rogue blast of power ebbed and finally disappeared, Bryan looked around the destroyed Council chamber in disbelief. What in the world had just happened?

* * *

Lysander arched his back when Roman drove deep, stretching his arms up and bracing himself against the headboard to keep from sliding up the bed. After a few more strokes, Roman's hips slowed, then stopped. He braced himself on his elbows and smiled down at Lysander. "It is time, my sweet mate. Are you ready?"

Lysander wrapped his arms around Roman's neck and nodded. "I'm ready."

Roman's voice deepened as he uttered the formal binding words. *"Do you freely agree to become my True Bloodmate, forging our souls into one, as fated by the Goddess, bonded together through eternity?"*

Lysander stared at him, realizing in that moment, how the next few minutes would abruptly change the course of his life. Awestruck by the solemnity of Roman's question, he could only whisper his yes. But it was enough.

Roman slashed his claw above his heart, tearing open a two-inch gash. "Drink Lysander. Drink deeply and join with me for eternity."

Lysander pressed his mouth to Roman's chest. As he tasted his first sip, Roman struck; his fangs piercing his neck, his mouth pulling Lysander's blood in large gulps. The initial pain quickly transformed into ecstasy. Orgasmic light exploded from his core, ran through his extremities and burst forth in an explosion that rocked the foundations of the world. Wind whipped through the room, tearing the sheets off the bed as rays of light flashed around, almost blinding in their brightness.

He clutched Roman to him, holding tight to keep from flying away as everything exploded around them. Roman's strong arms wrapped around him. He cupped Lysander's head, tucking it under his chin and held him close as they rode out the storm.

Awareness came back slowly. Roman slid to the bed beside him and brushed the hair back from his face, worry shining from his eyes. "Are you all right?"

"I'm fine. In fact, I feel amazing." Lysander reached over and clumsily patted him on the shoulder. "Why didn't you warn me bonding would be so explosive?"

"I had no idea it would be like that. I have never heard of such a thing." Roman frowned. "Though I do not believe that was only because of our Bond. Something else was going on." Roman gasped and took hold of Lysander's hand, holding it up where he could see it. "Your hand seems to be sparkling."

"What?" Lysander looked at it and blinked. "It's sparkling."

"I believe I just said that," Roman said dryly. "How do you feel?"

"I feel strange. Good, excellent even, but also different. It feels like there's energy bubbling under my skin, but that's from the bond. Right?" He looked at Roman questioningly.

Roman made a face like he didn't think so, before leaning over him and placing a hand on his chest. "Zander, I need you to do something for me. Close your eyes and try to see our bond. It should look and feel like a living line leading from you to me."

Lysander turned his focus inward, breathing deep, just like he did in his meditation class. Not that he'd ever been very good at it. Trying to keep his mind clear, he searched for the line Roman was talking about. Thinking his mate's name brought to his attention how good Roman smelled covered in both their scents. Then he heard someone yelling downstairs. What was that about? He wondered how many vampires actually lived here? He'd have to ask Roman later. Ooh. Was that bacon? Mmm, bacon. A BLT would be really good right now.

"Zander. You need to concentrate. Feel for the bond." His words may have sounded serious, but Lysander could hear the laughter in his voice.

Right, he was supposed to focus. It was really not the time to be wondering what would happen the next time they mated. Would it be as explosive or calmer? It would be fun finding out. He started to wonder if he could talk Roman into doing it again soon. Which somehow made him feel hungry. Seriously, a BLT would be awesome right now.

"Lysander!"

Whoops, right, concentrate. Lysander took a deep breath, held it for five seconds then slowly breathed out, sinking into his core. And quickly found a golden ribbon just waiting for him. Following it, he was led into a vast cavern filled with scenes that flashed before him as fast as lighting. He recognized Roman in various times and places. Whoa, these were Roman's memories. He moved through the cavern, past the memories, and found a glowing orb pulsing with red fire. Roman's core. He moved closer, basking in the warmth and brilliance as strands from Roman's core reached out and wound around him. Emotions filled him; joy, pain, so much pain and guilt, friendship, sorrow, and loneliness, a vast deep loneliness. His poor mate had lived with so much pain and loneliness through long centuries. Lysander made a vow then and there to make sure his vampire's life was filled with happiness and light.

But surprisingly, the most overwhelming emotion he could feel was love. But how could that be? Roman barely knew him.

"Not true. I can see who you are inside, Zander. And everything is beautiful."

Wait. Roman's voice was in his head. Could he do that? *"Can you hear me?"*

"Yes, I can, my precious Bonded."

"How is this possible?"

"We are Bloodmates that have True-bonded. We now have the ability to hear each other."

"Everything? All the time? Or is there a privacy switch?" Roman's laughter tickled his brain.

"Oh, Zander, you are so precious. Your mind is not an open book. You have to project your thoughts for me to hear you."

Whew. That was a relief. Lysander didn't want someone to have full access to his every thought. His mind was a messy and crazy place sometimes. He opened his eyes. "That was amazing. You are so strong inside and have lived through so much. I'm not sure if you'll be satisfied with just me."

Roman leaned down, giving him a quick kiss. "You forget, I saw all of you, just as you saw all of me. Your care for others and your capacity for love is boundless. You are perfect for me. It is I who is too old and cynical for you."

Lysander hugged him, squeezing tight. "Maybe we can be imperfect together?" Arms wrapped around him. "Now tell me how you can love me. We barely know each other."

Lysander looked up into Roman's face when there was no answer to his question, wondering at his sheepish expression. "Roman?"

"I may have, perhaps, followed you around after we first met."

Lysander pushed him back. "I knew someone was following me. I thought I had some crazy stalker."

"Well, you did have a stalker of a sort."

"Unbelievable. Do you have any idea how worried I was? And it was you all along."

"I am sorry. I needed to be near you. Once we find our mate, it is a built-in imperative to want to be close to them. With an incomplete bond, the drive to be close is even stronger. Since our first meetings did not end well, I also thought it best to get to know you better before I tried again."

"I'm sorry, Roman. I didn't know."

"Don't apologize. I know I was a bit pushy when we first met. After a thousand years, one achieves a certain level of arrogance, which unfortunately you did not respond well to. I just knew I needed to get to know you, so I pushed too hard."

Lysander stroked his face. "Well, I did think you were an asshole, but I wasn't much better. I don't like being pushed around and told what to do. After dealing with Mother all these years, I won't put up with it from anyone else."

"Yes, I understand now. Following you also allowed me the opportunity to see who you really are. How helpful and kind you are to those in need. How strong and loyal you are to your friends and brother. You are everything I could ever want in a mate. It was worth everything we went through to be able to bond with you in the end." He moved over to the edge of the bed, patting it. "Come sit by me. We have something important to discuss."

"More important than our mating."

"Not more, but important all the same." Roman faced Lysander, his knee pressing into his hip. Capturing his still sparkling hand, Roman brought it to his lips and pressed a kiss into his palm. "You were able to find our link when you searched. Did you notice anything else?" There was a knowing look in his eyes. Roman had realized something that he wasn't telling.

Lysander turned inward again and realized the energy he'd felt earlier was still bubbling inside of him. It hadn't dissipated in the least. His eyes snapped open. He turned to Roman who had an expectant look on his face. "I'm full of energy. And it's not because of the bond, is it?"

"It is not our bond; however, I believe it is related to it. When we completed our bond, the burst of mating magic must have unlocked your personal magic."

"I don't have any magic."

"You always had magic. It was only hidden away. But now that it has been unlocked, you will find you have a considerable amount of magic. Once you learn how to control it, I suspect you will be more powerful than any magic user before you."

Lysander reeled in shock. "The prophets were right." He clutched at Roman. "The prophets said that the greatest magic would come from me and would overturn the world. When I didn't have any magic, we assumed it would be my child. I have to tell Bryan." Lysander jumped off the bed in excitement. "Mother won't be able to use me to control him anymore. This is fantastic."

"Zander, slow down a moment. Think. Until you learn to control your powers, you are in even more danger from your mother. If she found out, she could easily control you, and through you, everyone else would be in danger. She cannot ever find out until you are able to protect yourself from her."

Lysander froze, knowing the truth in his words. "I'm bringing even more danger to your door."

Roman pulled him in tight. "Don't worry about that. I can keep you and the coven safe. You do not get to be my age and not learn how to survive power-hungry magic users. This is not the first time I have seen the drive for power corrupt. It is an unfortunate theme that has been repeated many times through the centuries."

Lysander relaxed into Roman's hold but his mind was spinning. He might not be sure he loved Roman, it being too soon for that, but he already felt fiercely protective of him. And while Roman might think he could protect everyone, Lysander knew his mother was not to be taken lightly.

Therefore, it was up to him to learn how to control his powers as quickly as possible. It was the only way to ensure everyone he loved could be kept safe from his mother and everyone allied with her.

Chapter Ten

Meanwhile, in the Council Chambers…

Bryan maintained tight control on his personal shielding as the Council members picked themselves up. He also kept a close eye on his mother, as she was his most dangerous and volatile opponent. The room was in shambles; every piece of furniture had been overturned, there were no pictures or hangings left on the walls, and the Council and his mother looked like they had taken a ride in a tornado. His protected area was the only untouched spot in the room.

The chamber's door opened, crashing against the inner wall when two acolytes rushed in. "Esteemed Elders. Are you alright? Oh Goddess, what happened? The whole building is a mess."

The acolytes quickly set about returning the room to order, helping the Council members to their feet and brushing off their robes, putting chairs and tables back in place. One of them ran out of the room, returning a few minutes later with a new pitcher of water and glasses.

But nobody assisted Charlotte.

Bryan kept a steady death glare on her, this last betrayal one too many. For while they were constantly at odds, they had managed to maintain an uneasy truce. Or rather, he had, for Lysander's sake. However, the moment she openly joined with Elder Ruth and raised her hand to attack him was the moment she had crossed his last line.

"Mother." He waited until he had her full attention. "As leader of Clan Galway, it is my responsibility to protect all members of our clan. I have been sorely negligent in my duty by trying to maintain peaceful relations with you when you should have been brought to task many times over for your manipulations and cruelty. Your actions today clearly illustrate where your true loyalties lie. Per my decree, as Clan leader, you are hereby banished from Clan Galway. Any inherited assets, either tangible or intangible, will be immediately forfeit. You may take only your clothes and personal jewelry you brought into your marriage. Any Clan heirlooms are forfeit, including your engagement and wedding rings. You may continue to use the Galway name for a period of three months, at which point you will revert back to your maiden's name. If you marry before that time, you will immediately refrain from using the Galway name and any associated connections to your former clan. As leader of Clan Galway, as witnessed by the Goddess, these are my wishes. As I will it, so it shall be." Bryan released the Galway Banishing spell, which only Clan Leaders had the power to use. As of this moment, nobody in the Galway Clan would recognize her as kin again.

Charlotte screamed. "You can't do that."

"It's done, Mother. You made your choices." Bryan turned to leave. "I'll give your best to Lysander." With those parting words, Bryan strode from the room, not looking back.

Charlotte was frozen, stunned by the events of the last few minutes. Banished? Who did he think he was? How dare he banish her? He had no idea what power she could gather against him. He would pay for this embarrassment. She would— What did you just say?" Elders Ruth and Thomas stopped mid-sentence. "Did you just say the power that tore through this building was because of a bonding?" Mouths moved, but neither spoke. "What kind of bond could cause that?"

Thomas sighed. "It's a closely guarded secret, privy only to Council members."

"I think we have bigger concerns. Someone just unleashed immense power against us. And you know how they did it."

Ruth looked at Thomas, who nodded, then explained. "When two paranormal beings of different classifications form a soul bond, it can result in unpredictable power or abilities. There's no way to know what capabilities and strengths will result. But mixed pairings who form a soul bond always produce such an outcome. The power burst we all just experienced was the result of a bond forming between a magic user and either a shifter or a vampire."

"You're saying that a magic user bonded with someone, which resulted in enough energy to tear apart this room. And they gain extra abilities as well? You are fools. Do you not see the possibilities? Why keep this information hidden?"

"You are a fool if you think common knowledge of this would help. How would we govern and control it if just anyone could mate across classifications and gain access to untold power or extra abilities? There is a reason this action is forbidden. Balance must be maintained." Ruth turned to other Elders. "We must find who did this and eliminate them immediately. I will reach out to the Assassin's Guild for assistance. The rest of you need to find out who this is and report back to me immediately."

Forgotten, Charlotte backed out of the Council chamber, a new plan coming together. If bonding could grant power of this magnitude, and she could hold control over the ones who gained it, she would finally have enough power behind her to have to overthrow these fools.

Because Bryan had been right about one thing today; the Elders had outlived their usefulness. She would soon correct that. Then she would deal with him.

* * *

The morning after…

"Thanks John," Lysander smiled at the vampire who delivered his breakfast. Digging into his plate, he moaned. "Roman, you have the best chef in the world. These pancakes are amazing."

Roman smiled. "I'll be sure to pass that on."

Waving his fork at Roman, he continued, "I need to meet with Bryan and let him know what's happened."

Roman glanced over his head. "That shouldn't be too difficult."

Bryan dropped into the seat beside Lysander, stealing his fork and helping himself to his breakfast. "Mmm, these are great. How do I get some?"

Roman signaled to John, waving his finger between the plate and Bryan. John nodded, walking through the swinging door to the kitchen. "They should be here shortly."

"Thanks, Roman." Bryan leaned back, looking the place over, checking out the roped off areas, which still showed some damage from the vampire attack. "I see the repairs are coming along nicely. How soon do you figure until you can open again?"

"Edgar thinks it will be another couple of weeks before we are ready to open. I wanted to ask if you have some way to shield the building from that type of enemy attack again? It is not good for business if I cannot keep my patrons safe."

"I'm sure I can come up with something. If I can work it into the building supports, I should also be able to protect it from natural disasters. Speaking of which," Bryan turned to Lysander, "have you watched the news yet? It seems an earthquake rocked the city yesterday. Scientists are at a loss and have no explanation for the phenomenon since it didn't register on any of their instruments. Certain areas of the city, like the Council building, were hit hardest and sustained the greatest damage." Bryan grinned at Lysander, who could feel his cheeks heat, then he snatched up Lysander's coffee cup and saluted him with it. "So, baby brother, anything you'd like to tell me?"

"How about you put down my coffee before I stab you."

Bryan snickered. "I was thinking more along the lines of explaining why you're sparkling."

Lysander looked at Roman, "I'm still sparkling?" Roman nodded. Lysander turned back to Bryan. "And you can see the sparkles?"

"I'm sure everyone can. You twinkle just like those vampires on TV." He took a sip of coffee then set the cup back in front of Lysander. "No offense, Roman."

"None taken." Roman pushed his chair back. "If you will excuse me, I will leave you both to talk." Lysander grabbed his hand, holding him in place. "Or I can stay."

Lysander proudly held onto Roman's hand and smiled at Bryan. "Roman and I completed our bond yesterday."

"Congratulations, Sandi. You too, Roman." Bryan stole Lysander's coffee again, laughing when he glared at him.

"Bryan something extraordinary happened when we bonded and after it was over, I suddenly had magic."

Bryan snorted into the coffee. "That's a bit of an understatement, Sandi. You're shining as bright as the sun." He leaned in, resting his elbows on the table, becoming serious. "Which is a problem. You've got too much power. Coming into it all at once, you didn't have a chance to learn how to control it and adjust to it as it developed. If you don't learn how to control it, and fast, you could seriously harm someone. I'll need to begin training you right away." He nodded thanks at John as he delivered Bryan's plate and a fresh cup of coffee, which Lysander immediately snatched.

At Bryan's glare he said, "You snorted in mine. You can keep it. I'm taking this one."

Bryan laughed, "Fair enough. Anyway, between you and me, we pretty much leveled the Council building." He shoved a forkful of pancake into his mouth, speaking around it. "By the way, I banished Mother."

"What?"

"She tried to attack me, so she's banished. Sorry, Sandi, I know you were hoping she would one day remember how to love you, but she only cares about herself. There's no bringing her around, she's just too far gone."

"I know, Bryan. It's okay. After the marriage fiasco, I realized she would never put us first. I'm only sorry you were forced to banish her."

"It had to be done. Once she sided directly with the Council and attacked me, I had no other choice."

"No You didn't." Lysander frowned. "You said you did something to the Council building. What was it?"

Bryan smirked. "Well, let's see. You started by blowing the place up with your power bomb, and I threatened to replace them…well, not so much threatened as I promised to replace them. It was a busy day for the Galway boys."

Roman choked back laughter when Lysander exclaimed, "Blew up the Council? How did that happen? We only had some minor shaking here, at least, I think that's all that happened." He glanced at Roman for confirmation, who nodded.

Bryan swallowed his pancakes, then grabbed his coffee, sipping it to wash down his food. "I suspect it's because the room was filled with power since Ruth and Mother were about to attack me. It'd be like filling a chamber with gas, then lighting a match. Magic calls to magic, so your surge of pure magical energy was drawn to the high levels of power created by Ruth, Mother, and myself. Fortunately, I had just put my shield up when your wave arrived and blew the place up. It was Epic."

"Holy crap. They're going to be coming for us hard in retaliation."

"Yes, and very soon. You broke the Council's rule for mixed bonding. Judging by the powers you gained, I totally understand now why it was forbidden. What better way to control everyone than to make sure nobody is strong enough to challenge them?" He ate another bite. "Our first order of business needs to be getting you trained up. At the same time, I need to solidify some more alliances. And we need to act on these quickly."

"I might be able to help with that. I can call on the coven leaders."

"Thanks, Roman. If we have the vampires on our side, that would be a huge advantage."

"Prince Roman, Prince Roman, the Council is here."

Two heads did a slow pan. "Prince?" Lysander asked.

Roman winced. "Perhaps I forgot to mention that minor detail."

"Prince." Lysander stood. "A Prince. What does that make me?"

Roman reached out to clasp his hand. "My beloved Consort, of course."

Bryan snickered.

"Shut up, Bryan. This isn't funny." Bryan just laughed. Lysander glared at Roman. "When were you planning on telling me?"

"To be perfectly honest, it slipped my mind that you were unaware."

"Being a Prince just slipped your mind? Are you kidding me with this?" He turned and punched his brother in the chest. "I said shut up." He sat down with a huff.

"Prince Roman, the Elders are waiting outside. They demand to see you."

Bryan immediately sobered. "They demand to see Roman? Now? In broad daylight?" he asked slowly.

The vampire wrung his hands nervously. "Yes, those were their words."

"Thank you, Jamie," Roman said. "Tell them I will be happy to meet with them tonight, once the sun sets."

Jamie hurried off to deliver the message.

Bryan grabbed Roman's arm. "Roman, you can't meet with them. Your bonding is forbidden. If they see you, they'll know you were the one to break the rule and they'll kill both you and Sandi."

"Kill Roman." Lysander jumped back to his feet. "They had better not."

"Uhm, Sandi, you might want to settle down."

"Yes, beloved. Please try to calm yourself. Fire is spurting from your fingers."

Lysander looked at his hand in shock.

Darkness' front doors suddenly burst open, letting in the morning sun. Vampires screamed, scattering as they dove for safety from the sun's deadly rays. Jamie's body came hurtling across the room, sliding along the floor with enough force that he vanished down the darkened hallway.

"Roman, get down!" Lysander shoved down on his shoulders, trying to push him under the table where he'd be protected, growing more frantic when the morning sun's rays bathed Roman's body. Panicked, he threw himself at Roman, knocking him to the ground, covering as much of his mate as he could with his smaller body.

"All is well, Zander. I am unharmed," Roman said, sounding bewildered.

But how could he be? This was the sun. Cursing when he saw how much of Roman was still exposed, Lysander tried to make himself as big as possible to cover as much of his body as he could, terrified at what the sun was doing to his mate.

"Beloved, stop. I am fine."

Lysander propped himself up so he could glare down at Roman. "What do you mean you're fine? You're covered in sunshine. It's going to burn you alive."

"And yet, it is not. I am not hurt."

"What?" Lysander sat up, his eyes widening. He patted Roman in wonder. "Holy crap. You're not burning."

"As I tried to tell you." Roman stood, bringing Lysander with him. "It would seem our bonding has given me the ability to walk in daylight. An advantage I will put to good use immediately." Roman's fangs dropped and claws extended from the ends of his fingers. "I believe I will have a chat with these magic users who broke into my place and endangered my vampires."

He flew across the room in a blur of speed, moving so quickly that Lysander didn't see him until he crashed into the crowd of magic users outside the main door, his claws slashing whoever he could reach.

A crossbow bolt narrowly missed Roman's head, embedding itself in the doorframe behind him. "Oh no, you didn't." Lysander raced to help Roman, Bryan right beside him.

"That's him. That's the lawbreaker. Kill him."

Lysander didn't recognize the woman pointing at him, but thought he heard Bryan say Ruth. Not that he had time to worry about that. Movement across the street caught his eye. Looking up, he saw a weapon being pointed at them. Or more specifically, at Roman. Panicked, he reached out with his hands as if he could physically stop the bolt from coming. But instinct took over and the magic coiling in his center rushed to the surface, exploding from his fingers in a fiery ball of fury. It roared across the street, gaining mass as it traveled, until it reached the hapless assassin and incinerated him in seconds. Unfortunately, it took out the corner of the building as well.

"Lysander, look out." Something heavy crashed into him, knocking him to the ground. A sharp thud drew his attention to the bolt quivering in the wall right where he'd been standing. "Are you okay?" Roman asked, his worried gaze running over his body.

"I'm good, go. I'll find Bryan and stay with him."

Giving him a last look, Roman nodded and took off.

Lysander scrambled up, searching for his brother, and spotted him exchanging fireballs with three other magic users. He started toward him when he noticed another magic user sneaking up behind Bryan's unprotected back. Lysander flung one hand at the threat, this time trying to control the focus of his magic. Which seemed to work. The magic-user went up in a towering pillar of flame, but he managed to avoid setting fire to Roman's building or any of the hiding vampires.

"Roman, Lysander," Bryan yelled. "Pull back and get behind me. I'll cover you."

Lysander dodged incoming bolts and spears of flame as he scrambled to get behind Bryan. Roman appeared beside him a moment later.

Once he saw they were behind him, Bryan raised his hands, putting up a shield blocking the doorway and open sections in the walls. Crossbow bolts and fireballs struck it, falling harmlessly to the ground. Bryan then motioned with his hand, which must have done something to shield as the light passing through it changed, looking more blue and less bright.

Bryan turned to Roman. "I've blocked the sun's rays. It's safe for your vampires to come out now."

Roman inclined his head. "Thank you."

Bryan nodded. "Are you both all right?"

"We're good, Bryan." Lysander hugged him. "Thank the Goddess you were here. They would've killed all of Roman's coven if it wasn't for you."

"I'm glad I was here too, Sandi." Bryan held him at arm's length. "You didn't do too bad using magic for the first time, but we really need to work on your control. You could have burned down the whole block." He pulled him in for another hug, squeezing tightly. "You scared the hell out of me baby brother. The first thing you're going to learn is how to shield yourself, got it?"

"Yes, Bryan."

"Okay." Bryan stepped back, then frowned at Roman. "Why didn't you stop them yourself? I know you have enough ancient power you could have leveled them. You didn't actually need me here."

Roman looked mortified by Bryan's question. Lysander had no idea vampires could blush, particularly Roman.

"I am embarrassed to admit that once I realized I could withstand the sun's rays, I may have let that thrill overshadow my common sense. I wanted to deal with them personally. To put my hands on them and show them their error for daring to attack my home and family. I wanted them to feel my wrath." He turned to Lysander. "I am sorry, my beloved. My reckless loss of control could have cost you your life."

Lysander didn't think so, not with Bryan there to keep an eye on him, but it was easy to see Roman was kicking himself for how he'd dealt with the situation. Maybe he could smooth it over. He smiled and rested a hand on Roman's chest. "It's okay. I completely understand. Sometimes emotions get the best of us."

Roman drew himself up. "I am not a juvenile vampire. My emotions do not control me, I control them. I cannot afford to let my desires drive my actions. Self-control is an absolute necessity when you reach my age."

"Roman, look at me." Lysander needed to stop this spiral Roman was on. "I get you could have and perhaps should have, used your power to drive them away. But you have a new ability. You also had Bryan here as backup. This was the perfect time to use that ability to vanquish your enemies. Nobody got hurt and if your vampires had been at greater risk, I have no doubt you would have flattened everyone with just a thought. The need to get personal and make them pay for hurting your family makes perfect sense to me." He grabbed his shirt collar, bringing their faces together. "I'd much rather have a passionate and impulsive mate than a tightly wrapped, restrained one. You can keep me safe and still loosen your self-control, showing your spontaneous and emotional side. In fact, I insist on it."

"No. I cannot allow—"

He attacked Roman's mouth to stop him, hopefully illustrating the joys of spontaneity over rigid control. They separated when Bryan started fake coughing behind them. "Do you mind? We were having a moment."

"I get that, Sandi, but I need Roman's attention." Turning to Roman, Bryan said, "You have a couple of problems. The Council shouldn't have been able to track down the magical anomaly that quickly. The only reason I was able to follow it was because the power signature reminded me of Sandi. Nobody else on the Council is familiar with him, so they had to have found out some other way."

Roman stiffened. "What are you implying?"

"I'm saying someone close to you fed them that information."

"None of my vampires would betray me like that."

"Are you willing to risk Sandi's life on that? They had to find out some way and the only ones aware of your bond are in this building." Bryan walked behind the bar to get a bottle of water. He cracked the seal, then pointed the bottle at Roman. "But the biggest problem is that the Council and their minions now know about you two. They'll have issued a kill order, so we need to come up with a plan to keep you both safe."

Roman nodded, his face growing cold. "How long can you shield the bar? Is there a way to permanently keep them out?"

Bryan tossed his empty bottle in the recycle bin. "I can tie off the shield, but that will prevent anyone from being able to come or go while the protective barrier is up. And given enough time, the Elders will eventually break through."

"That is not a practical solution. Max, get over here. We need to come up with some better ideas."

Chapter Eleven

Bryan and Lysander walked into the drawing room at Galway mansion, discussing various upgrades they would need to make to the house and surrounding land to make it safer. Bryan stopped just past the doorway. Lysander paused when he saw who was there, then continued into the room to get a good seat for the upcoming entertainment.

"Mother. What are you doing here?"

"This is my home. I live here."

"Not anymore." Bryan went to the sidebar and poured a glass of water. "You were banished. You should have already packed your belongings and left."

"You can't do that. This has been my home for over one hundred years." Charlotte's scowl had no effect on him.

"It used to be your home and now it isn't. This estate belongs to the Galway family, to which you no longer belong." Bryan drained his glass, then poured another. "Can I get you anything, Sandi?"

"I'm good, thanks." Lysander watched his mother closely. She was trying to keep up a good front, but he could see the cracks. Her shock at Bryan's dismissive behavior was crumbling her normally icy control. Like a cornered animal, this is when she would be her most dangerous.

Bryan turned to Charlotte. "You have one hour to pack your belongings. After which time, I will have you forcibly removed from the premises. But be advised. Albert will be checking your bags before you are allowed to leave. We wouldn't want any Galway heirlooms to end up in your luggage by accident."

Charlotte stalked over to Bryan, fury in every line of her body. "How dare you treat me like a common criminal? I am your mother. You will show me respect."

"How dare you, Madam?" Bryan yelled back, slamming his glass down. "You joined with the Council in attacking your own child. Your first-born son. My father's heir. Leader of this clan. This, after years of manipulation and threats against Lysander. You are no mother and haven't been since Father died." He turned away from her. "Now, you are no one."

Charlotte stared at his rigid back. Lysander saw when she finally comprehended she had gone too far in her bid for power. Turning a frosty glare on him, she left the room. The slam of the front door a few moments later let them know she had left.

"Are you okay, Bryan?" Lysander asked quietly. "That can't have been easy for you."

Bryan sighed. "I'm more worried about you. I gave up on her years ago.

Lysander went over to him and hugged his stiff body. Bryan was obviously more upset than he wanted Lysander to know. "It'll be okay. I have Roman and I have you. I don't need her. Not anymore."

* * *

Lysander walked through the door to Roman's new office space, sauntering lazily past Max and Edgar. He threw a smirk over his shoulder, mostly just to annoy Edgar, then straddled his mate's lap and gave him a hungry, I'm happy to see you kiss.

Max cleared his throat. "I guess we're done for today." He grabbed Edgar and started pulling him toward the door. "We'll be back in the morning."

"But I still need him to sign off on the repairs to Darkness," Edgar complained, dragging his heels. "I've been trying to get his attention for days. Things were much more efficient around here before he became…" The door closed, muting the rest of his complaints.

"Good day, my beloved. Did you need something?" Roman raised an eyebrow when Lysander gave him his best innocent expression, obviously not buying it.

Lysander grinned. He did love to poke at Edgar, who monopolized Roman's time like a dragon hoarding treasure. Interrupting a meeting was a guaranteed way to annoy Roman's assistant. "I just wanted to see how your vampires were settling in?"

He'd come up with the brilliant idea—if he did say so himself—of temporarily moving Roman and his vampires into the mansion as it had space to house the entire coven with room to spare. It also had inherent protections spelled right into the foundation. With some fine tuning from Bryan, they now controlled who had access to enter or leave the property, making it a safe haven for everyone. Bryan had also polarized the windows in such a way that the specific rays of the sun that were harmful to the vampires were blocked, but still allowed light to shine in. But the most important advantage to Lysander was the protected magical training area. Bryan had been working with him on his control, and the magically enhanced walls and shielding were benefiting everyone, as Lysander tended to blow things up on a regular basis. His control was coming, but it was a slow process.

"They're adjusting well. Thanks to your brother, the coven is safe and I have this space to run my businesses."

Lysander looked around what had formerly been his mother's study. It was a much cozier and welcoming space since Roman had taken it over. Antique statues spanning the last few centuries had places of honor. Roman had also added a few paintings to the wall. A place that used to elicit dread now felt comfortable and welcoming. Especially when Roman was in the room.

"How are the magic lessons coming along?" When Lysander hesitated, wondering how much to share, Roman tipped his chin up, so he could look him in the eye.

Lysander smiled nervously. "So, as it turns out, I have much better success in accessing my powers when I act on instinct. I'm having a considerable amount of trouble releasing the magic under controlled circumstances." Lysander turned away, mumbling, "I might have almost exploded Bryan today."

Laughter caused Roman's chest to vibrate.

Lysander's attention snapped back to him. "It's not funny. I could have hurt him."

"You would not have done so."

"You don't know. You weren't there."

"Tell me what happened?"

Lysander blew out a breath, the frustration from that moment coming back. "I couldn't get anything to work. No matter how hard I tried, I couldn't access my magic. Bryan kept pushing and pushing until I finally lost my temper. If he wasn't so fast at defensive magic, I could have killed my own brother."

"He was never in any danger."

"But—"

"My sweet Bonded. Bryan knows exactly what he is doing. He was only pushing you to see if he could break through whatever is holding you back."

"You really think so?"

"I know it for a fact. Bryan came by earlier to discuss how today's lessons went as he thought you might be upset. You should remember he is always prepared. You will not be able to injure him."

Lysander nodded, then licked his lips. "Can I tell you a secret?"

"Always."

"This power scares me." Lysander sank into the comfort of Roman's arms as they wrapped around him. "It's so vast, sometimes I feel like it'll overwhelm me. Adding in the fact I have to learn how to use it quickly, I'm worried I won't be able to control it and I'll hurt someone I care for. What if I hurt you?" Lysander's voice grew fainter as he continued. "My biggest fear is what if I choke up when I really need to access it and you or Bryan are injured?"

"Lysander, you will be fine. You are strong and resilient. I have faith you will master this."

"How can you say that?"

"You forget, I have seen your heart. I know what drives you. How determined you are to succeed. But your fear is holding you back. Once you accept and embrace your power, submit to it, I am sure you will find a way to control it." Roman leaned down, kissing him gently. It quickly turned carnal, as was normal in the early days of bonding.

He pulled back, smiling at Lysander. "Would you like to come with me so I can demonstrate the power you gain from submission?" Roman waggled his eyebrows.

Lysander laughed at his uncharacteristic silliness, feeling much better all of a sudden. Which had probably been Roman's intent. Playing along, Lysander gave him a counteroffer. "I have a better idea. Let's see if you can get us to the bedroom before I get your shirt undone. Loser bottoms."

The sound of Lysander's laughter rang out through the house as Roman carried him there in a dizzying burst of speed and motion.

* * *

Lysander was lounging on the bed, skin still buzzing in satisfaction, watching Roman as he fastened the last button on his cuffs. Jinx jumped up on the bed, tail lashing, obviously still in a snit from being locked out of the bedroom. Lysander tried scratching under his chin, but got whapped by a paw in return. He snickered when Jinx turned his back on him and started cleaning his fur. He was such a princess sometimes.

"Zander, the guards I've assigned will be waiting outside the door."

Lysander frowned, turning to Roman. "What guards?"

"Your personal guards."

"I don't have any guards."

"As of today, you do."

"But I don't want any guards."

Roman sat on the bed next to him. "My precious mate, you are my heart, my very life." Roman's words filled him with joy. Too bad he had to keep talking. "Your safety is of utmost importance to me. I need to ensure you are protected when I'm not around. Which is why I have assigned two of my best enforcers to be with you at all times."

"But we're living in the mansion. I never go out. Why would I need guards here?"

"Some of the staff may still be loyal to your mother. I cannot have you at risk in your own home. I spoke with your brother and he agrees with me."

"Bryan knew about this?" Somebody was going to be very sorry for not warning him.

Roman nodded. "I voiced my concerns and made him aware of my intention to keep you protected."

"I think you might be overreacting. Besides, I don't want people following me around all day long."

Roman leaned in and gave him a sweet kiss. "Please, my Consort. Do this for me. I need to know you are safe at all times." Another long drugging kiss followed, fogging his mind until he found himself agreeing.

"All right. If it will make you happy."

"Thank you, beloved. I appreciate your sacrifice."

As he left the room, Lysander realized he had just been played. He looked over at Jinx. "Did you know about this guard thing?" Jinx still refused to acknowledge him, focused on cleaning a spot on his leg. Lysander flopped back on the bed. So now he was traveling with a posse. Terrific. He pulled a pillow over his face and vented his frustration.

* * *

Exhausted, yet pleased with the results of today's practice session with Bryan, Lysander headed to Roman's office, Jinx meandering beside him, his ever-present posse following a short distance behind them. Passing a couple of vampires, he was startled when they bowed to him. Slowing, he looked over his shoulder. They were still bowing. His guards nodded to the bowing vampires, who then stood up. What was up with that?

Frowning, he continued down the hall. Passing one of the ballrooms, he looked in on a group of vampires and some of the mansion staff setting up tables.

Turning to his guards, he asked, "Do you know if there's a meeting coming up?"

They looked blankly at each other.

"Never mind. I'll check with Roman." Turning back to the room, he saw the vampires had halted their work and were now bowing to him. The humans looked at the vampires, then bowed in his direction as well, though with much less grace. Seriously, what was going on?

He whispered back to his escort. "Why are they bowing to me?"

"On the Prince's orders, Consort."

Really? He'd just see about that. Lysander picked up his pace, hoping they didn't run into anybody else. All this bowing was unnerving.

He managed to reach Roman's office without crossing anyone else's path, which was a relief, though short-lived, when the two enforcers guarding the door bowed. Damn it. Everyone needed to stop doing that.

"Consort." The vampire on the right banged his fist over his heart then opened the door to Roman's office. "The Prince is waiting for you." Lysander gave them a cursory nod, then rushed through the door, leaving his guards outside. Jinx streaked past him to flop down in the sunny patch in front of the French doors.

"Zander? Is something wrong?" Roman hurried around his desk. He cupped Lysander's cheeks, kissing him thoroughly, then brushed his damp bangs back from his face, dropping a quick peck on his forehead. "Talk to me. What has you unsettled?"

"Why is everybody suddenly bowing to me?"

"Oh, that." Roman stepped back, returning to his chair behind the desk. "I have instructed the entire coven to show you proper respect, as befits my Consort."

"Well, tell them to stop. It's freaking me out," Lysander said, sitting on the edge of Roman's desk.

"That I will not do," Roman said decisively. "You are my Consort, my fated Bloodmate. Things have become too lax around the coven and it is time everyone was reminded of their place in the hierarchy. You are next in line, deferring only to me, and will be shown all the respect and courtesies deserving of your position."

"Roman, I don't want anybody bowing to me." Lysander placed his hand on Roman's shoulder. "It makes me uncomfortable."

"You will have to get used to it." He crossed his arms stubbornly. "I will not be changing my orders."

Lysander pulled back, ready to unleash his anger, then saw the fear in Roman's eyes. Something more going on here than Roman suddenly deciding to be all autocratic. Then it hit him. "Is all of this because you haven't discovered how the Council found out about our bonding?"

Roman's eyes filled with anger. "Of course, it is. Someone in my own coven betrayed us. My people, whom I protect and shelter, and one of them betrayed me. Betrayed us. They will all be reminded of who holds the power of life and death over them. The betrayer will rue the day they acted against me."

Lysander snickered. He tried to hold it back, but really. "Rue the day? I'm surprised you didn't shake your fist in the air."

"This is not a joke, Lysander. You could have died in that attack."

"No, you're right. I'm sorry." He patted his angry vampire's arm. "But Roman, you can't punish everybody for the actions of one or two people. That's not fair."

"A prince does not need to be fair. Only obeyed."

"Yes, my Prince." He snickered at the look he got. "Maybe we can exempt your inner circle from bowing. The thought of Max and Edgar doing so is just weird." Lysander hesitated, tilting his head. "Actually, I like the thought of Edgar having to bow to me. Never mind."

"I am glad you agree. Perhaps we can now close that discussion." Roman pulled him onto his lap, nuzzling his hair.

Lysander snuggled in. The discussion was far from over, but it could wait until a later time. He may have to put up with guards, but he was definitely not going to have people bowing to him. Except for perhaps Edgar. That he could learn to enjoy.

* * *

Charlotte paid her informant, then pulled her hood further over her head. Glancing furtively around, she quickly made her way to the end of the alley then hurried down the sidewalk.

Stupid boys. Thinking they could kick her out of her own home. They had no idea of the people and resources she had at her disposal. Today's transaction had brought her one step closer to the one she sought. Soon she would have her revenge. Everyone would all pay for slighting her.

Starting with her disloyal sons.

Chapter Twelve

Lysander put the finishing touches on a charcoal drawing of Jinx he was making for Roman's office. He'd captured Jinx as he'd been the day he'd first seen Roman, hissing and growling at the vampire. Lysander snickered to himself as he shaded more attitude in Jinx's eyes, imagining his vampire stoically hanging the drawing on his office walls then pretending it wasn't there.

Though Roman was learning to loosen up somewhat, he had a ways to go, there still being far too many times where he was uptight and aloof. It was a work in progress but a lot of fun.

He made a last stroke on the page, then held it out. Perfect. Roman would love it. Actually, Roman was going to hate it, but since he usually indulged Lysander, he'd hang it up anyway. And then find a sexy way to punish him for winding him up. Lysander was quite looking forward to seeing what Roman came up with.

Setting his sketch pad down, Lysander stretched, loosening muscles tight from being hunched over too long. He tended to lose track of time when he was focused on a project. His stomach growled, which made him realize he was starving. That's when he noticed the tray that had been left by the door. He hadn't even heard his lunch being delivered.

Feeling lazy and wanting to test his developing magical skills, he decided to see if he could bring his lunch to him. Concentrating on the tray, Lysander held out his hand and tried to visualize if levitating. He suddenly laughed as a movie scene popped into his mind. Lowering his voice, he said, "Use the force, Lysander," and focused on it again.

Then almost had a heart attack when the tray lifted a couple of inches before crashing back to the table. Holy crap. He might be onto something here. He focused again. The tray shakily rose, dipping down a couple of times before rising smoothly. Concentrating hard to keep it level, Lysander pulled it towards himself, smiling when it drifted lazily through the air in his direction.

There was a sharp knock, then the door opened.

Lysander jerked in surprise, which caused the tray to veer sharply off course and crash into the person who'd come in. He winced when he saw Edgar standing there, dripping with water that had filled the pitcher now laying broken at his feet. Lysander's sandwich slowly slid off of Edgar's shoulder and dropped to the floor, separating when it landed and smearing mustard over his Italian leather shoe. His chocolate pudding had somehow landed on Edgar's head and was now oozing down the side of his face.

Lysander felt a bubble rise up from his stomach. He tried holding it back, but to no avail. Laughter burst from him as he took in the mess he'd made of Roman's normally impeccably groomed assistant. He laughed harder when he looked into Edgar's stormy eyes, and saw the promise of his death in them.

Gasping, trying to control his laughter, he finally calmed enough to ask, "You wanted to see me about something?" Narrowed death eyes started his laughter again, until Edgar turned and stomped out of the room, slamming the door behind him. Lysander fell off his chair and curled on the floor, howling, until he was finally laughed out. Intermittent chuckles kept bubbling up as he laid on the carpet staring at the ceiling. What a wonderful day it was turning out to be.

* * *

Visiting Carlos' coven…

"Carlos." His head shot up when his Second addressed him. "I've got a visitor for you." He pushed a woman to her knees in front of Carlos' throne. "Bow before your betters."

"I will not prostrate myself before the likes of you." Pushing to her feet, the woman shrugged off the vampire trying to hold her, arrogantly raising her chin at Carlos. "I've come to offer you an alliance."

Carlos, slouched on his throne with his leg dangling over the side, studied the woman, who was vibrating with fury. Her pale blonde hair was pulled back in some fancy design only women understood and she dressed in a navy business suit. A strange choice of attire when meeting with a vampire. Carlos held her eyes for a long moment before pulling a knife from his boot. He extended his claws and proceeded to clean them with the tip of his knife, leaving her stewing in mounting frustration. Deciding enough time had passed to make his point, he returned his blade to his boot and addressed the woman, who by now had her teeth clenched so tightly his own jaw ached in sympathy.

"An alliance, you say?" Carlos sauntered down from his dais and circled the woman. "You smell familiar." Inhaling deeply behind her ear, he parsed the pheromones she exuded, relishing the fear he could scent. "Yes, I've smelled this before, perhaps from someone close to you." He scratched a fang along the side of her neck, greatly enjoying hearing her whimper, and tongued up the drops of blood trailing from the wound. He stepped back, smacking his lips and humming. "What do you know of my little mouse who escaped?" Her eyes squinted in confusion. Carlos waved his hand negligently. "No matter. I will reclaim him soon enough." He sauntered back to his throne, once again slouching casually, pleased with the potential his afternoon suddenly offered. Waving his hand in a circle, he urged, "Tell me of this alliance you're proposing."

* * *

Magic lessons at the mansion…

"One more time Lysander. Focus."

"Focus he says," Lysander muttered. "What does he think I've been doing? I'm going to focus on him being shoved through the wall in a second."

"You need to concentrate, Lysander. Try harder."

Flinging his dripping bangs from his face, Lysander scowled at his brother. "I'm trying as hard as I can. You keep telling me to wrap my will around my power. What does that even mean? I don't know what my will feels like. How in the hell am I supposed to wrap it?" Frustrated, he kicked his water bottle across the room.

Bryan came over, taking his hands. "Let's try this. Close your eyes. Take a deep breath, hold it, now blow out and let the stress flow from your body. Another one. Good. Now concentrate on your core, your center. It's the source of

140

your magic. It's like a sphere of pulsing light. Can you see it?" At Lysander's nod, Bryan continued. "I'm going to find my core and wrap my will around my power. You won't be able to see it, but if you stretch your senses, you may be able to feel what I'm doing, how I shape the magic. That might help you understand what I'm talking about."

Lysander focused on his core of power, then pushed his awareness toward his brother, much like when he flowed along the bond tying him to Roman. He floated on his power searching for Bryan's presence. At last finding what he assumed was his brother's aura, he pushed, sinking through. He let his power guide him to Bryan's core, then tried to feel what Bryan was doing. There was an initial resistance, so he pushed harder, abruptly breaking through a barrier. There. This was it. He could see how Bryan was manipulating his magic, the way he was tying the strands together. Lysander pushed closer, focusing to emulate Bryan's actions, doing the same with strands of his power, then joining them to Bryan's.

An explosion rocked the room. Opening his eyes, Lysander saw everything was engulfed in flames. The entire cavernous room was filled with the fires of hell except for the small bubble sheltering Bryan and him.

"Lysander, what did you do?"

"Me? I didn't do anything," Lysander said, growing panicked at the look his brother was giving him. "I swear. I didn't do anything."

"Dear Goddess." Bryan grabbed the front of his shirt, shaking him. "Do you even understand what you did?"

Batting at Bryan's hands, he yelled, "Nothing, I already told you, I did nothing. This wasn't me."

Bryan clamped down on his shoulders. "Stop it. Look at me." As Lysander stilled, Bryan gazed at him, awestruck.

"Sandi, you linked your powers to mine. Somehow, some way, you linked us. I didn't even know such a thing was possible. In fact, I don't think it is, but it's the only explanation." Waving his hand through the air, Bryan closed his fist, snuffing the flames. Big showoff. "This is amazing. This might be the very thing that saves us."

"If you say so." He was still a little freaked out by the whole thing.

"I do. This may just win us the war, Sandi." Bryan grinned at him, excitement beaming from his face. "Once we figure out how you did it, we'll practice until we can link at will. Then when we need it, you'll be able to feed me power, increasing my own, and I'll control our combined magic and use it to our best advantage."

Lysander nodded, quickly catching on to what Bryan was suggesting. This really could give them a better chance if they had to battle the Elders.

Bryan grabbed his hands. "Let's try that again. Close your eyes and focus, reach for my core."

Taking a deep breath, then letting it out, Lysander closed his eyes, once again flowing with his powers.

"Good, Lysander. Now watch as I control the flow."

* * *

Lysander was sitting on his mate's lap, having snuck into the office when Edgar had stepped away for a moment. He'd come to see Roman the moment he'd finished training with Bryan so he hadn't had a chance to change out of his sweaty clothes. Roman didn't seem to mind, pulling him onto his lap the moment he got near enough. Jinx had followed him and was currently basking in the sunshine from his favorite place in front of the French doors that led to the garden.

"How was today's session with Bryan?"

"It was amazing. Bryan and I had a real breakthrough. I made so much progress. I'm feeling much better about our chances if the battle with the Elders actually transpires."

"That is wonderful to hear. I know how much this has worried you, though I never doubted for a moment that you would figure it out." Roman's long, graceful finger pushed a lock of hair behind Lysander's ear. "I also have good news to share. I have reached out to the other coven leaders and have most of their support. There were a few holdouts, but those are only minor covens, with brash, young leaders. They will learn their place."

"Of course, your Highness."

Roman flicked his nose. "Do not be impertinent."

Lysander laughed, then grew serious. "And Carlos?" The nightmares of his torture under Carlos' hands were becoming less frequent, but he still saw dangers in the shadows.

Roman growled. "Carlos had better hope I never see him. I will rip his head off and present it to you as a gift."

"Umm, gross. I can just torch him instead."

Roman chuckled, pulling him close. "As you wish. But be aware, my precious mate, the moment we are done dealing with the Council, I am hunting down Carlos. He will pay for what he did to you with his life."

"I'm fine with that, but not the head, please. I don't need that." Lysander shuddered.

"As you wish."

Lysander couldn't wait for the day his torturer met his end. After Lysander had been rescued and healed, Roman had led an enforcer squad to Carlos' hideout but the place had been empty. No sign of the vampire or his followers remained, with the exception of the manacles that had been used to imprison Lysander. They'd been left hanging from a hook driven into the doorframe of the main entrance, mocking Roman for being too late. Bryan had told him Roman had been so enraged, he'd ripped them free and ground them into dust with his hands.

Needing to drive thoughts of Carlos from his head, Lysander took advantage of this rare moment alone with his mate and pulled Roman into a kiss. His hands tangled in Roman's long, silky hair as he took control of the kiss, knowing it would trigger his mate's aggressive nature. And it did.

Roman growled his displeasure and quickly took charge of the kiss. He picked Lysander up, adjusting him to straddle his legs, and hungrily devoured his mouth. Small nips on his lips drew blood that was greedily sucked off. Roman's tongue delved to the back of his mouth, his hands holding Lysander's head, adjusting the angle to his satisfaction as he fed from him.

Moaning in pleasure, Lysander started grinding against his tight stomach. Tearing his mouth free, he tilted his head to the side, excitement filling him when Roman nosed behind his ear, licking his skin before biting down. Passion exploded. He rode out the wave while Roman fed, prolonging his pleasure, then let out a contented sigh and collapsed against his mate's chest when Roman licked the small wound closed.

"My precious mate, you are so good to me," Roman whispered, nuzzling his temple before resting his cheek on Lysander's head.

Lysander just sighed, enjoying the quiet moment in his mate's arms, still buzzing with satisfaction. It truly fed a deep need in him to be able to give his blood to Roman, knowing he was keeping his mate healthy and strong.

A knock on the door interrupted their stolen interlude. "Prince Roman, Mage Bryan would like a moment."

Yeah, these formal titles were weird and had to stop. Lysander reminded himself he needed to open that discussion again soon, whether Roman liked to or not.

"Give us a moment." Roman looked at Lysander. "Can you do your thing?" He waved his hand in a circle.

Lysander snorted. "Of course." One of the fun things he'd discovered and practiced until his execution was flawless was the ability to clean Roman and himself up with magic. After one of their passionate interludes, it only took a small burst of power and focus of his will and they could be squeaky clean in seconds.

Smiling his thanks, Roman called out. "Send him in." Lysander sat up, positioning himself to sit sideways on Roman's lap. Bryan crossed the room, a knowing smirk on his face. Lysander flipped him the bird. Bryan laughed and sat in one of the now comfortable chairs on the other side of the desk. It was yet another change Roman had made from the flimsy, hard chairs his mother had used.

"Good, you're both here." Bryan leaned his arms on the desk. "I've just got off a call with my magic user friends, Nick and Alex. They've confirmed what we suspected. The Council has called out a feud against Clan Galway and Roman's coven. If we cross into anyone's territory, the Council has ruled we are to be held, by whatever means necessary, until they can come and deal with us. The clans have also been advised they will not be held accountable if they are required to use extreme prejudice in following the Council's orders."

"That sounds terrifying. Everyone will be trying to kill us."

Bryan chuckled. "You would think so, wouldn't you? According to Alex, only the oldest magic users and any of Mother's previous alliances are openly supporting the Council. Nick and Alex are reaching out to everyone to see who we can count on as allies in our fight against the Elders. Which seems to be almost everyone as most of the clans don't trust the current Council. Apparently, a lot of the clans have been dissatisfied with the Elders for some time."

Jinx strolled across the room to sharpen his nails on Bryan's chair. Bryan leaned over to pick him up, settling him in his lap. Loud purrs filled the air as Bryan scratched under his chin. Grinning down at the cat, Bryan continued. "It also seems that the Elders are running into some resistance with the vampires." He smiled at Roman. "According to Nick, most of the coven leaders are unavailable whenever the Council calls. Their loyalty is clearly with Roman, so there shouldn't be many vampires in the upcoming fight."

"That's great news," Lysander said.

"Yes. The bad news is that we're definitely looking at paranormal battle. If we want to minimize the damage, we're going to need to control when and where it happens."

"How are we going to do that?"

"That's what we have to figure out."

"This could be devastating for humans if it gets out of control," Lysander said. "Has anybody reached out to the shifters? They should be made aware of the upcoming battle."

Bryan shook his head. "It's hard to figure out who's in charge of the shifter packs. Other than the Alpha's of the individual packs, they don't have an established hierarchy. And from what I've heard, even the ruling Alphas are in a constant state of flux due to ongoing leadership challenges. The Elders have been refusing to help them establish any kind of controlled ranking system, claiming it's pack business, so the shifters have been left to their own devices. With the constant changeovers in pack leadership, the whole thing is a complete mess."

"Shit."

"Exactly," Bryan said, stroking Jinx's back. "I have my suspicions the Elders have orchestrated the shifter power struggles as a means to control them. I think the best thing for now is to keep them out of the upcoming battle. Afterwards, when we restructure, we can help them establish proper ruling Alphas. They should also have representation on the new Council."

"Bryan, you're talking about a coup." Lysander was shocked. He couldn't believe it had come to this.

Bryan nodded. "We've been heading in this direction since I first threatened the Elders. Their attack on Roman's bar pretty much sealed the deal on how this would play out." His solemn expression held determination. "We're going to war, baby brother. There's no turning back now."

"This is all Mother's fault. None of this would be happening if she hadn't been so power hungry."

"I'm not sure if that's true. After speaking with Alex and Nick on what they've seen and heard, it's easy to see the Elders are corrupt and have been abusing their positions and power for a while. They're not guiding or supporting any of the paranormal communities like they're supposed to. It was only a matter of time before someone would revolt. Mother's shenanigans just hastened the timeline and ensured our direct involvement." He shrugged. "Luckily for us, we have a secret weapon they're unaware of." He winked at Lysander.

* * *

Charlotte watched from a shadowed corner as her contact came closer. Her eyes locked on the package held casually under his arm. "Do you have it?"

"That depends. Do you have my money?"

Charlotte kicked the duffle by her feet then held out her hands. "Give it to me."

A voice roughened by years of living hard, laughed at her. "Since you're so eager, I think my price just doubled."

Charlotte glared. "Luckily for you, I understand the lack of honor shown by men of your ilk. I have already placed double our agreed upon price in the bag. Now, give me the package before I get angry."

He thrust it into her waiting hands, eagerly grabbing the duffle and opening it to check the contents. Charlotte left him to it, turning away and carefully pulling back the wrapping on the object she held. She gasped when she finally laid eyes on what she had been seeking for so very long. The millions of dollars she had paid for this was nothing. There was always a way to get money. But this. This was priceless. A jewel beyond measure. With this, nobody would be able to stop her.

The cocking of a gun broke her absorption with her prize. Turning, she saw her contact holding a pistol, the muzzle pointed directly at her head.

Motioning with the weapon, he stated, "I'll just be taking that back. I have another buyer to meet."

"You don't seem to realize who you're dealing with. Unfortunately, you will never be able to make use of the lesson I'm about to teach you on the risks of not honoring your agreements."

With a small motion of her fingers, webs of power wrapped around the ruffian's throat, choking him. She gazed with dispassionate eyes as he fell to the cement, his heels drumming on the ground and hands clawing at this throat as he thrashed out his final moments. When his body finally stilled, she gracefully stepped over his motionless form, leaving the duffle of money behind. It was inconsequential. Let the rats watching from the shadows fight over it. She had the only item of value. With what she held, she would finally be able to rule them all.

Chapter Thirteen

Edgar stared him down, arms crossed. "No. You're not going in."

"I am going in so you'd better move out of my way, Edgar." Lysander crossed his own arms, mimicking Edgar's stance. "I've barely seen Roman in the last few days."

"Prince Roman is extremely busy. Not only does he have many business interests that require his attention, he now has to mobilize the vampire covens for this war your family started."

Lysander rolled his eyes. "Give it up, Edgar. I know that you can handle his business requirements in your sleep."

"Well, yes, I suppose I can," Edgar agreed. "However, that doesn't change the fact Roman is too busy to see you right now."

"Let's just see about that." Lysander called out through the closed office door. "Roman, do you have a minute for me?" When the door immediately opened, he smugly sauntered past a fuming Edgar.

"Consort." Turning to the guard, he saw him holding out the parcel he'd brought for Roman. He'd completely forgotten about it during his run-in with Edgar. Nodding his thanks, he relieved the guard of the package and strolled over to Roman.

"Beloved, how can I help you?" Roman swiveled his chair toward him.

He placed his package on the desk, then climbed into his mate's lap, tucking his nose into Roman's neck and breathing him in. He'd missed him the last few days, with Roman's time being taken up with strategies and planning. Which was hard on Lysander as he was finding it difficult to function if he couldn't be near mate. The few hours they had together before dawn wasn't adequate to soothe the ache he felt in his soul. Or satisfy the compulsion driving him to constantly seek out his mate.

Assuming these needs were a peculiarity of the mate bond, he resolved to find time to discuss it with Roman. But not today. Today he wanted to give Roman his gift and enjoy whatever time he could get with him.

Lysander snuggled in closer and tilted his head back. Roman followed his silent request, his mouth landing on Lysander's lips, which eagerly parted for Roman's kiss.

"Prince Roman, I must protest. I have this time blocked to discuss coven matters."

Lysander smiled against Roman's mouth. He had to give props to Edgar for continuing to fight even when the battle was thoroughly lost.

"Hmm?" Roman continued kissing him, pulling him closer.

"Prince Roman!"

Lifting his head, Roman blinked at Edgar. "You were saying?"

"Prince Roman. We have important matters to discuss. Your Consort can't just walk in here and monopolize your time whenever he wants."

Did Edgar just stamp his foot? Oooh, he was seriously pissed.

"And yet, that's exactly what I did." Lysander smirked at Edgar, who's face tightened with anger.

"Zander, play nice."

"I don't want to. He always acts like he's in charge of you. It's a fight every time I want to see you. You're my mate, not his. I don't like having to go through your guard dog just to spend time with you."

"I will talk to him. But please try to work with him. Edgar has been looking after me for many centuries and he's feeling a bit displaced by the changes.

Damn it. Now Lysander felt awful. *"Fine. I'll try, but I make no promises we'll ever be friends."*

"If you can find a happy balance, that will suffice." Aloud Roman said, "Edgar, give us thirty minutes." He looked to Lysander. At his nod, he continued, "When you come back, bring Max. We have a few final details to cover off."

"Yes, Prince." Edgar stomped to the door, closing it firmly behind him. Roman sighed.

"I'm sorry. I really will try harder. I didn't think about how he felt." Lysander grimaced. "I may also be a bit jealous of him having so much of your time."

"My darling mate, I will always make time for you. Now, what did you need?"

"A couple of things. First," he grabbed the package and handed it to Roman, "I have a gift for you, or rather, your office."

Roman looked at him in wonder. "Thank you."

Lysander snickered. "Don't thank me yet, you haven't seen it."

"Since you made it for me, I'm sure I will love it." Roman unwrapped the packaging and paused upon seeing the drawing. Lysander watched the small tic in Roman's jaw when he clenched his teeth, before he forced a smile. "It's Jinx. How lovely."

Lysander couldn't hold in his laughter any longer. "It's okay, Roman, you don't have to hang it in here."

"No, it will hang in a place of honor. After all, I come to work every day with his fur on my favorite suits. Why would I not want to see his friendly face staring down at me? All day long."

Lysander collapsed against his chest, laughter bubbling uncontrollably, enjoying his mate's droll sense of humor. Roman shut him up with a kiss, but only after accidentally dropping Jinx's picture into the trash. No problem. He'd pull it out later. There was a spot on their bedroom wall where it would fit perfectly.

Long moments passed in pleasurable kisses before Lysander recalled his second reason for being there. He pulled back, fiddling with Roman's top button. "I received an email from my landlord today. I need to make a decision on what I'm doing with my apartment."

"And what have you decided?" Something in his tone had Lysander looking up. He looked hurt. Why would Roman, oh? Oh. Realizing what was upsetting his vampire, Lysander grasped his cheeks, pressing their foreheads together.

"Roman, whatever you're thinking, stop it right now. I'm not going to keep it. I still have the apartment because I haven't even had a chance to pick up my things yet. Everything has been in such an uproar since we met." Lysander kissed him on the nose. "I need to decide what to do with it, mostly my things. I'm not sure if I should have them brought here for storage or..."

"You will live with me, so your belongings will be moved into my rooms at the coven."

"All right. I just wanted to check with you first, since your home is already fully furnished."

"Your home is with me for the rest of your life. You should be surrounded by the things that make you happy. Including your cat." He couldn't quite hold back his shudder.

Lysander laughed. "Then all we need to decide is if it's best to leave everything at the apartment until the issues with the Council settle down, move it all here, or have it sent to Darkness."

"I see." Roman thought for a moment. "Perhaps it would be best to keep your apartment for a bit and leave your possessions where they are. Darkness is still undergoing repairs and we do not want to have to move everything more than once. It is also not safe for you to be wandering around from place to place. I won't have you at risk."

"Ahh, you do care about me," Lysander teased.

"Lysander, you are my very life," Roman said seriously. "Without you, I would not survive. I love you and need you near me at all times."

"Oh, Roman," Lysander hugged him tightly around the neck, "I love you, too. I'm sorry I haven't told you already."

"I know you do. I can feel it in your words and sense it through our bond; however, hearing you say the words makes my heart sing." Roman tightened his arms. "Now let me hold you until Edgar and Max arrive. I have missed you these last few days."

There was no other place Lysander would rather be.

* * *

A few days later…

Lysander grabbed Roman's arm. "Stay with me this morning."

Roman leaned down, kissing his forehead. "I wish that I could, but we are meeting with Bryan's mage friends, Alex and Nick, today."

"But I hardly get to see you anymore. Surely you can postpone your meeting for an hour or two."

"Unfortunately, I cannot. Planning for war is a time-consuming business."

"How about I come with you then? I haven't seen Alex and Nick for a while."

"Why not have a nice lie in, then you can spend time with Jinx in the garden later in the morning."

Lysander frowned. He was starting to feel like a child being sent off to play while the adults did grown-up stuff. "I think since I'll be participating in the fight, I should be a part of the planning."

Roman smiled down at him. "Today is about boring strategy discussions. No need to put yourself through that. You should relax and enjoy your day." He got another kiss on the head, then Roman left the room.

Lysander scowled at the closed bedroom door. Roman better stop blowing him off or they'd be having words. Lots and lots of words.

* * *

"Bryan, I'm telling you, something is wrong with Roman. I feel like he's avoiding me. I can never get in to see him anymore and when he comes to bed, he falls right to sleep. He's hardly even letting me feed him. I'm starting to get worried."

"I'm sure everything is fine. Every relationship has to go through an adjustment period. That's probably all this is."

Lysander shook his head. "No, that's not it. I can feel him distancing himself through our bond. Something is going on."

"Why don't you try talking to him about it?" Bryan looked at his watch. "Sorry, Sandi, I've really got to run." Bryan clapped him on the shoulder before rushing away.

Lysander glared at his retreating form. Did Bryan not hear him just say that Roman was avoiding him? How was he supposed to talk to him if Roman wasn't ever around?

* * *

Lysander was hiding in the gazebo in the North Garden. People rarely came this way, so it was perfect for someone who wanted to escape. He needed a break from the rising tensions in the mansion. As preparations continued for the upcoming battle, everyone was getting more stressed and tempers were flaring.

He sighed, putting down his sketch pad. His mind was blank. He couldn't find escape in his art, which had never happened to him before. He was really starting to worry. The strange distance between Roman and himself was growing worse and he didn't know how to fix it. It had come to the point where he wanted to spend every waking moment with Roman, but whatever time he had with him was never enough. He was always driven to get closer. It felt like the bond was alive and needed proximity to Roman, but wasn't finding whatever it was looking for. Lysander had tried discussing it with his mate, but Roman would just assure him everything was fine then go to his next meeting.

But everything was not fine. He just didn't know what to do about it.

An incoming call interrupted his gloomy thoughts. Glancing at the display, he smiled when he saw Tommy's name. "Hey, Tommy. How are you?"

"How am I? I'm fine. I have a better question. How are you? You just disappeared. You're never home, you haven't called. I never see you out with anyone. What's going on, Ell? Why are you ghosting me?"

"Oh shit, Tommy. I'm sorry. There's been so much happening. I didn't even think to call you."

"You didn't think to call me? I thought I was your best friend." He sounded hurt.

"You are my best friend, Tommy. You and Richie are the brothers of my heart. I'm sorry if I hurt you. I have no excuses. It's just—" His voice petered out.

"What's going on, Ell?"

Lysander sighed. "It's a long story. Do you have time right now?"

"I always have time for you."

Which was more than he deserved after hurting his friend. "All right. Here goes. It all started that night I met you at Darkness…."

Lysander spent the next hour catching Tommy up.

"Let me get this straight. You met your fated mate, who's a vampire Prince, you suddenly have major magical powers, you almost got married to a woman, you were captured and tortured by an enemy vampire, you started a war with the Elders, so now everyone wants to kill you, and you're in lockdown at your mother's mansion, which is now your brother's, since your mother has been banished from the clan. Did I miss anything?"

Lysander groaned. "Nope, that pretty much covers it."

"Holy shit. No wonder you didn't have time to call me. You're totally forgiven." Tommy started laughing. *"What do you have planned for next month?"*

"Don't even joke about that. The way things are going, I'm afraid to even think about it."

"Ell," Tommy's voice got serious, *"you've been trying to hide it, but I've been your best friend for too many years. Something else is wrong. What's up."*

Lysander's voice cracked. "I don't know, Tommy. Something's wrong between me and Roman. Every time I bring it up, he just pats me on the head and says everything is fine. Fine. Goddess, but I hate that word."

"Sounds like you need someone to talk to. Is it okay for me to come over, what with you being locked in and all?"

"That would be awesome. I'd love to see you. I'll let the guys covering the gate know you're coming. But hurry. I could use a friendly hug."

"I'm leaving right now. See you in a few minutes."

Lysander ended the call then messaged security to warn them of Tommy's arrival. Excitement filled him as he rushed from the garden, heading to the front gate so he could be there when Tommy arrived. He hadn't realized until now just how much he'd missed his friend.

"Tommy," Lysander called out, running towards him with his arms outstretched, ready to hug the stuffing out of him.

"Ell!" Tommy shouted back and charged toward him. Just before he reached Lysander, the guards tackled Tommy to the ground, rolling him to his stomach and yanking his arms behind his back.

"What are you doing? Get off of him." Lysander pulled on random arms, trying to get them to move. "Tommy, are you alright?"

"I'm good." Tommy's voice came faintly from underneath the guards who still had him pinned.

"I said to get off of him." Lysander's anger rose when the guards didn't listen. His hair started whipping in the breeze that had suddenly risen up. "Let him up now." Sparks of flame erupted from his fingertips.

"Consort. Please don't. They are only following the Prince's orders."

Lysander turned to see one of the guards from the gate running over to him. "Explain."

"Nobody is allowed to touch the Consort unless first approved by the Prince. The penalty for doing so is death. They were only protecting you."

"From my best friend? I don't need to be protected from him."

"Then think of it as them saving your friend's life. If he had managed to reach you, the guards would have followed the Prince's orders and killed him."

Lysander paled. "What?"

"I'm sorry, Consort. The law is that nobody is allowed to touch the Consort, unless permitted by the Prince. Breaking that rule is punishable by death."

Shock turned quickly to fury. Someone had some explaining to do. He turned to his two personal guards, who had finally let Tommy up. The glare he leveled on them had both guards wincing and looking away, refusing to make eye contact. Good. They should be worried after attacking his friend. Looking Tommy over, he was glad to see he was unharmed. "I'm sorry, Tommy. I had no idea that would happen."

"It's fine, Ell. I'm glad your Prince is so protective of you."

"Yes. Let's go have a talk with him about that, right now."

Turning, Lysander stormed toward the mansion, flames still flickering at the ends of his fingers. Tommy and the guards followed a few feet behind him.

Arriving outside Roman's door, the guards made motions to stop his entrance.

"Do not interfere."

"But Consort, the Prince said…"

"I don't care. Move or I'll move you." They looked at each other, then quickly stepped to the side.

Lysander was too angry to try the knob, instead choosing to blast the door from its hinges with his magic. Stepping into Roman's office, he realized he had interrupted a meeting Roman was having with Bryan, Max, Edgar, and another man. Too bad. He was too furious to wait for them to finish.

"Beloved?" Roman stood up, coming around the desk. "What's wrong?"

"Don't you beloved me. Explain why your vampires attacked my best friend."

Roman looked at the guards assigned to him.

"He was going to hug the Consort."

"Ah, I see. Thank you." Roman turned back to Lysander. "No one is allowed to touch you. The guards were just doing their job."

"Tackling my best friend to the ground and restraining him is not doing their job. They had no right."

"They had every right. They were following my orders. Nobody is to touch you."

Lysander glared at him. "Then change your orders. Tommy is my best friend and if I want to give him a hug, then I'll give him a hug."

"Then he will die."

Lysander froze. "What did you just say?"

"Anybody who touches you without my permission dies by my order."

"Then change your order."

Roman crossed his arms, staring down at him. "No."

Lysander was outraged. "You do not get to dictate who I can or cannot hug. You are my mate, not my owner."

"I am your Prince. You are my Consort. It is my right to protect you how I see fit. You will follow my orders in this. That is my final word on the subject."

Lysander was so furious he could barely see. Squinting, he spoke softly, forcing Roman to strain to hear him. "I may be your Consort, but you will not control me. I have already lived a life under someone's control, abused by their power over me. I will not live that life again. Not even with you."

Roman's expression changed, growing horrified when he realized what Lysander was saying. "Beloved—"

"No!" Lysander's hand slashed through the air, too angry to listen to any apologies. "When you pull your head out of your ass and are ready to talk to me as an equal, come and find me. Until then, I don't want to see you." With that he stormed from the office, leaving behind a stunned and silent group.

* * *

Roman stared at the empty doorway. What had just happened? Turning and looking at the men sitting behind him was no help. They looked equally stunned. He walked over to his desk and collapsed into his chair. What had he done? How did he even start to fix this? The look on Lysander's face when he accused Roman of being like Charlotte would haunt him for the rest of his very long life.

"Roman," Max spoke to him softly. "Perhaps you should talk to him. Tell him why."

He shook his head. "You heard him. He doesn't want to see me right now. I have to respect that and give him time."

"Don't give him too much time. You will both suffer from being separated."

"I know, but he needs some space right now. As do I." He'd been keeping secrets from his mate and he knew he'd already strained their relationship. Roman rubbed his heart. His mate's new anguish coming through the bond was making it hard to think.

"Your Consort is strong and brave. Congratulations on your mating, my old friend."

"Thank you, Marcus."

"Do you think it's wise to allow him to disrespect you like that? If others—"

Roman held up his hand. "Marcus, we've been friends for over five hundred years. I caution you to not continue down this path or you will become my enemy. My Consort's strength and bravery has allowed him to survive and overcome a life that would have damaged and broken many. Lysander's inner strength has allowed him to thrive. He is kind and selfless and honorable. I am proud he is mine. That he is secure enough in himself to stand against me defending a friend is why I love him deeply. No one is allowed to tarnish his name or speak out against him. Nobody. Not even a valued friend."

"Forgive me, Roman. I congratulate you on finding your perfect match."

"Thank you." Roman looked around the room. "Gentlemen, we are done for the day. Max, come with me please." Roman strode from the room."

Chapter Fourteen

Lysander paced from one end of the room to the other, ignoring the guards banging on the door. He'd locked them out and used magic to prevent their entry. They were lucky he hadn't lit their asses on fire for hurting his best friend.

Still fuming, he muttered under his breath. How dare Roman treat him like a child, ordering him around and expecting him to obey mindlessly. Never again would he allow himself to be disregarded like that. Especially from the one person who was supposed to have his best interests at heart.

Turning to make another circuit of the room, he bumped into Tommy, who stood in his path.

"Ell, do you think you might be overreacting a bit?"

He glared at Tommy. "No, I don't think I am. I should have equal say in this relationship. I am not a child who has to do as they are told. Roman needs to understand that. I will not allow another person to control me."

Tommy held his hands in the air. "Okay tiger, slow down. I just want you to think about this. I saw a man acting from fear and overprotectiveness." He paused. "And perhaps stubbornness because you publicly confronted him. I don't think he wants to control you, Ell, just keep you safe. You really should talk to him after you've had a chance to cool down."

Lysander shook his head. "No. He said he would have you killed. I will not back down from this. He's in the wrong and needs to change his rules."

Tommy nodded. "You may have a point. I don't want to die, so thanks for not letting him kill me."

"You don't have to thank me for that." Lysander sighed. "I can't believe any of this is even happening. I had no idea your visit would turn out this way."

Tommy snickered. "After everything you've experienced the last few weeks? I wouldn't expect anything else from you."

Lysander laughed until he cried. Tommy pulled him into his arms, holding him tightly while he'd cried out all of his anger and hurt. Eventually, the emotional storm subsided.

"Better now?" Tommy patted his back until he nodded. "Good. Let's watch a movie. Something with car chases where lots of shit gets blown up. I don't know about you, but I've had enough emotional drama for one day." Tommy looked down at his shirt, grimacing. "And get me a rag or something. You got snot all over my shirt."

Lysander snorted and dragged Tommy over to the couch. Mindless T.V. with his best friend sounded perfect.

* * *

Lysander relaxed back into the couch, stroking Jinx's fur, his rumbling purrs helping soothe his aching heart. Tommy had left a couple of hours previously, so he'd had nothing to distract him from the chaos of his thoughts.

His eyes slid over at quiet tapping on the doorframe. "Go away, Bryan. I'm not in the mood to talk to anyone."

"I know." The asshole walked in anyway.

"What do you want?"

"I came to see how my brother is doing."

"I'm fine. Go away."

Bryan chuckled softly. "Yes, I can see that. Why is your cat draped across your neck?"

"Because he wants to lie there."

"Do you always let him do whatever he wants?"

"Yes. It makes him easier to deal with."

"Huh. So, if you tried to make him do something that was for his own safety, how would he react?"

"Bryan, do you have a point you're trying to make?"

"Perhaps. Sandi, you do realize Roman's not really like Charlotte."

"I know that. But he can't just overrule me and try to force me into doing whatever he thinks is best. I don't care that he's a thousand years old and I'm only twenty-seven. He didn't even listen to me or acknowledge my feelings. I need to be an equal partner in the relationship or it's not worth having."

"Sandi, he was only trying to protect you."

"I understand that. It's why I agreed to have guards and live in the mansion. That does not give him the right to kill my best friend or to overrule me when I vouch for Tommy. If he wanted a doormat, he should have made somebody else his Consort. I will never let someone rule over me that way again."

"I don't think he feels that way." Bryan sat on the edge of the couch. "He had some pretty amazing things to say about your strength and resiliency after you left. He was prepared to end a five-hundred-year relationship in support of you. He really loves you, Sandi. You have to talk to him. There has to be a reason for why he reacted like he did."

"I know, Bryan. I just need time to get over the hurt and anger. Please let it go for now."

"Okay. Do you mind if I just sit with you for a bit?"

"Sure." Lysander continued to stroke Jinx's fur, his brother's silent support easing some of his pain. He hoped Roman could go a few days without needing his blood. As much as he needed time to come to terms with his hurt and anger, he didn't want to cause any harm to his mate.

* * *

"Roman."

"Yes, Max?"

"Don't you think it's time to go home?"

"Not yet. I can feel that my Consort is still deeply troubled. His mind is in turmoil. I want to give him more time."

"All right. But not too much longer. You need to feed soon."

"I know. I promise not to wait too long. You do not need to worry, Max."

Max sighed. "And yet, I do."

Roman ignored him, focusing on his bond with his mate, trying to be with him in the only way possible right now.

* * *

Lysander sighed, then answered his phone. "Hey, Tommy."

"Hey, Ell. How are you holding up?"

Lysander rubbed his aching chest. "I'm not going to lie. I've been better."

"Have you talked to him yet?"

"No."

"You need to talk to him. You're hurting both of you hiding like this."

"I know, Tommy, but I don't know what to do. I can't face life with a mate who won't listen to my feelings or give my decisions consideration. I'm not sure I'm ready to face him and find out he intends to overrule me for the rest of my life."

"I don't think he wants to. You need to give him a chance to explain or you'll both die a miserable death. I don't want to lose you, Ell. You're my best friend."

Lysander was shocked. "What are you talking about? I'm not going to die."

"Your brother told me that the longer you and Roman are separated, the greater the strain there is on Roman, increasing the chances of him turning feral. If he can't be brought back, they'll have no choice but to kill him, which will also kill you. I don't want that to happen, so go talk to him right away."

"Dear Goddess. I didn't even consider that. That might explain why I feel worse every day."

"Probably. Please promise me you'll go see him before it's too late."

"I will, Tommy. I promise."

"Good. I'll hold you to that." Tommy suddenly snickered. Lysander waited, his years of being friends with Tommy letting him know what was coming. *"Try to keep me abreast of the situation."*

Lysander chuckled. "At least you didn't say boobs this time."

"Shut up, Ell. You need to stop giving me shit about that." He hung up.

Lysander laughed. Not likely. That was never going to get old.

* * *

Lysander sat in the window seat, staring morosely at the gardens in the fading light. A sharp rap on the door startled him from his gloomy thoughts.

"May I come in, Consort?"

"Now's not a good time, Edgar."

The door edged open. "Please, Consort. It's important."

Lysander regarded him thoughtfully. Edgar's whole body was pleading for entrance. Not a look he'd normally associate with Roman's super efficient assistant.

"All right. You can come in for a bit." Edgar walked in, bowing to Lysander. "Edgar, please don't bow to me."

"Prince Roman has ordered that all must bow to his Consort, no exceptions."

"Yeah, well, that's going to be changed. No more bowing."

"If you insist, Consort."

"Maybe stop with the Consort, as well."

"That I cannot do. It is a title of great honor, for a position of power that goes back to the beginning. In giving you that title, Prince Roman is showing that he holds you in high esteem, and that all must defer to and respect his Consort. That title you will not be allowed to change. To do so would be to dishonor the Prince."

"Oh. I didn't realize. I thought it was just a formality. Thanks for explaining." Lysander got up, moving to the couch. "I'll show better appreciation for the title in the future. I don't want anyone to think less of Roman due to my actions.

Edgar frowned. "I don't understand. Your current actions reflect very poorly on Prince Roman. You are making him appear weak. Were you not aware of that?"

Lysander inhaled sharply. "No. I wasn't. Damn. Roman must be so disappointed in me."

"I believe he is more disappointed in himself. But yes, you should be aware that all of your actions reflect on Roman, good or bad."

"And this is bad." Lysander nodded his head. "Okay, Edgar, I appreciate you letting me know. I have some damage to make up for."

"You're welcome, Consort." Edgar tipped his head. Lysander sighed at the deferential gesture, but chose not to comment.

Lysander leaned against the back of the couch, closing his eyes. "Edgar, I've had a lot of time for self-contemplation over the last several days. I've done a few things I'm not proud of and I owe you an apology. I've been an ass to you since I bonded with Roman. I was jealous of you and your relationship with him, so I poked at you out of spite. I'm sorry for that."

"Well, damn." Edgar dropped down beside him. "How am I supposed to hate you now? You've gone and ruined all my fun."

Lysander turned his head to look at Edgar. "You hate me?"

"Well, no, but not for lack of trying. Roman was mine to look after first. I've been with him a long time. You were an interloper who made my life much more difficult." Edgar sighed. "However, I've never seen Roman this happy before and the joy you bring him makes it hard to hate you." He chuckled. "I did give it my best try though."

"Except I'm not making Roman very happy right now."

"No, you're really not. But I have hopes that you'll eventually get it through that thick head of yours that Roman only wants what's best for you and to keep you safe. You're making the both of you miserable for no good reason."

"You're right. Thank you again for telling me how it really is." Lysander hesitated, then held out his hand. "Truce?"

Edgar looked at him a long time before his lips quirked. He reached out and shook. "Sure, why not? Truce."

They sat silently for a moment, enjoying their newfound peace with each other.

"Why did you come here, Edgar?"

"I have a story to tell you."

"Okay. Did you want anything to drink before you start?" When Edgar's eyes widened, Lysander snorted. "We just said truce. Does it really surprise you I would offer hospitality?"

"Yes, actually, it does. Our truce is seconds old." Edgar chuckled. "You're a better man than I, Consort. And I would love a water. Get one for yourself too. You might need it."

Lysander got off the couch and went to the kitchen to grab a couple of bottles of water. Edgar being here worried him. He knew this story was about Roman and he was nervous about how bad it had to be to have compelled Edgar into taking the initiative to talk to him. Returning to the living room, he handed Edgar his bottle and retook his seat. "Okay. I'm listening.

Edgar leaned his head on the back of the couch and looked at the ceiling. "Once upon a time, there was a young vampire named Roman."

"Really, Edgar? A fairy tale."

"Hush, I'm telling a story. This young vampire had an older brother named Nico, whom he looked up to and loved very much. Nico was an amazing older brother and took young Roman under his wing. He taught him everything he knew about honor, integrity, and compassion. He taught him how to hunt, how to feed, and how to use his vampire abilities. He also taught him how to rule. See, the young vampire was Prince to his brother, who was the King. King Nico ruled over his people with all of the honor, integrity, and compassion he had taught his younger brother." He stopped to take a drink of his water, sniffing.

"Edgar?" Lysander questioned softly.

"Let me finish. I can only get through this once. One day, King Nico found the most beautiful vampire princess who turned out to be his fated Bloodmate." He paused at Lysander's quick intake of air. "Yes, Nico was also blessed by the Goddess. However, there was a snake in his kingdom. A snake that was jealous and wanted the King for herself. A snake that pretended to be the best friend of the princess, so she was trusted and granted privileges not allowed to many. A snake that was accepted into the bosom of the royal family. One day her lust for the king turned into hatred for her rival. In her rage at not being able to have the King for herself, she stabbed the princess in the heart, killing her instantly."

"Oh no, dear Goddess, no."

"The king, overcome with grief and dying an agonizing death due to the loss of his Bloodmate, turned feral." Edgar turned to Lysander. "Who do you suppose had the responsibility to put down the King when he lost himself to his madness?"

Tears streamed down Lysander's face as he shook his head. "No, please tell me it wasn't Roman."

Edgar nodded. "He had to kill his own brother, whom he cherished and loved above all others. To save many innocent lives from the king's madness, he had to put him down like a wild animal." Edgar paused to take another drink, brushing a hand over his eyes and sweeping away the gathering moisture. "That is the day Roman put the rule into effect. Unless the Prince himself approves, to touch his Consort means death. Until he can look into a person's heart and read their intent, nobody will be allowed near you. For your safety and for his."

Lysander had to turn away, shedding tears for the rage and pain Roman must have felt. When he had himself mostly under control, he reached out and took Edgar's hand. "Thank you for telling me. Poor Roman. I can't even imagine how much he suffered."

Except…he could. He'd felt Roman's intense pain when they bonded. A pain and sorrow that stretched back for centuries. One he still carried with him. "Edgar, did Roman's brother have long blond hair and blue eyes?"

Edgar looked surprised. "Yes. How do you know that?"

"I've seen him in Roman's memories. He still carries the loss and guilt to this day."

Edgar's hand tightened on his. "Lysander, you have to help him. He's carried the burden long enough. Help him to forgive himself so he can remember and grieve the brother he loved, not the animal he had to destroy."

"I will. Thank you again. I hope one day we can be friends. I think you'd make a good one."

Edgar tilted his head, looking at him strangely. "As do I," he said slowly.

After Edgar left, Lysander started thinking of a way he could bring peace to his vampire's wounded soul.

***

"Roman."

"Hmmm." Max's voice cut into Roman's deep contemplation. Though his link with his Bonded was growing weaker, he was still able to feel his precious mate. He was sad, but he also felt purposeful. Roman assumed he was deep in his art, using his craft as a means of coping with their separation. He was hopeful that Zander would agree to see him soon. He missed his mate dreadfully.

"Roman, are you listening to me?"

"Sorry, Max. I was not. How can I help you?"

"I think it's time you went home."

"Max?"

"No, Roman. It's been days. Enough is enough. We have a war to plan for. You need to go to your room and straighten things out with your mate. You've both had enough time to get over your hurt feelings. You can't solve anything if you don't actually talk to each other."

"Are you kicking me out?"

"For Goddess' sakes, you're a Prince, not an adolescent schoolgirl. Suck it up, make peace with Lysander, and get back to leading our people." He stormed out of the room.

Roman watched Max leave, surprised by the ass kicking his Second had just given him. Apparently, he was going home.

***

"Are you just about done with the pity party, Consort?"

Lysander set his glass of water on the counter before turning. "Max. That's not what this is about."

"That's exactly what this is about. You're pouting because you didn't get your way."

"That's not what I'm doing."

"Yes, it is." Max yelled. "You didn't get your way, so instead of dealing with it like a grownup, you're hiding in your room making Roman suffer for a crime he didn't commit."

Lysander got right in his face. "He was going to have Tommy killed."

"Only if he broke the rules, which he didn't. Tommy's fine. You're fine. But Roman's not. You're punishing him for something he didn't do. It has gone on long enough."

"I am not punishing Roman. I needed time to come to terms with the fact he wouldn't listen to me or respect my wishes. That he thinks I am less than him."

"There's something you need to understand, Consort." Oh goodie, the sneering was back. "Roman is a prince to our people. He has to be strong, decisive, and confident in order to keep us safe. He has managed to do so for centuries." Fingers were now poking into Lysander's chest. He leaned backward over the counter, but they followed him. "You are undermining that confidence, all because your feelings are hurt." Max stepped back a pace, then turned to walk to the door.

"That's not..." Lysander began before the asshole interrupted him.

"It's time you grew up and started acting like a Consort. If you want respect, earn it. Show everyone why you deserve it. We are on the cusp of war. Instead of preparing for it, Roman is losing faith in himself and putting all of our lives at risk. Pull your head out of your own ass and stop hiding like a child having a temper tantrum because he didn't get his way. Be the Consort Roman deserves. Goddess knows, he doesn't deserve to be treated like this."

That did it. Max had gone too far. Power rose up in Lysander. Max went flying across the room and smashed into the wall beside the doorway, before dropping to the ground.

"Max." Lysander ran over to him. "Are you alright? I'm sorry. I didn't mean to do that."

Max groaned, rolling over onto his back. Pushing himself up to lean against the wall, he looked Lysander in the eyes. "Did I strike a nerve? Are you finally hearing me?"

Lysander stopped to think. Was he punishing Roman? He'd thought he was trying to come to terms with his feelings but now he wasn't so sure. Max's words might possibly have some merit. Not that he'd ever admit it to the asshole. But it was true that this had gone on long enough. He needed to discuss his feelings with Roman, all of them, because staying apart wasn't helping either of them. And the pain from their separation was starting to hurt him physically. He could only imagine what it was doing to Roman.

"I'll talk to him." Lysander offered Max a hand up. After a slight hesitation, Max took it.

"Good. By the way, that was a nice punch of power. It's about time you showed some of the fire that first caught Roman's attention."

Lysander looked at him in amazement. "You're happy I threw you across the room?"

"Well, not happy, but it gives me hope you'll stand up for our people instead of hiding away like a child."

Lysander rolled his eyes. "You've made your point, Max. I get it. You can drop it now."

Max nodded. "Good. I expect to see you at the next strategy meeting."

"I'll be there."

Nodding a final time, Max strode from the room.

Lysander looked at his hands. He'd thrown Max across the room with barely a thought. He grinned. That was freaking awesome.

Chapter Fifteen

Roman knocked softly on the door to his and Zander's suite.

The door opened immediately. "Roman." His mate looked pleased to see him. He prayed to the Goddess that meant Zander had forgiven him.

"May I please come in?"

"Of course. We should talk."

Hoping for the best, Roman stepped into the room, and was reminded of the first time he'd visited his mate when Jinx came out of the bedroom and hissed at him before retreating. Goddess help him, but he had missed that damn cat as well.

Roman sat on the couch, waiting for Lysander to join him. Once he did, Roman took Lysander's hands in his.

"Lysander, I owe you an apology. In fact, I owe you many." He shook his head when Lysander opened his mouth. "Please, let me finish. There is much to explain."

Lysander nodded. "I'm listening."

"I am not sure the best place to start." Roman turned Lysander's hand over and rubbed his thumb back and forth across his palm. "First, I must apologize for damaging our bond." At Lysander's sharp intake of breath, he nodded before continuing. "You were correct. There was a distance growing between us. The fault for that lies with me."

He patted Lysander's hands, then gently set them in his lap before standing and facing him. "You see, I was worried about how you would react if I have to go into my battle frenzy state. You had a horrifying experience with Carlos that still gives you nightmares. I do not want you to ever see me that way. I could not stand it if I made you afraid of me."

"Roman, I trust you with my life. How could you ever think I would be afraid?"

"It is not an unreasonable assumption. A battle frenzy state looks very similar to a vampire going feral. In fact, if a vampire does not maintain control of himself or the battle rages on for too long, it is easy to slip from frenzy to feral."

"I have faith in our bond. You will always know me, Roman, so I have no doubt I could bring you back. I will never be in danger from you. Your soul speaks to mine."

Roman was overwhelmed by Lysander's complete faith in him. However… "There is more." Roman took a deep breath. "My greatest concern was how you would feel if I were to kill your mother. Chances are good that she will be a part of the upcoming fight and there is always the possibility that I will be the one to end her existence."

"Roman, I would never…." Lysander paused, then frowned.

Roman waited while he thought it through, greatly relieved his mate was taking his concern seriously. He would not have had faith in his response if he had answered too quickly, without giving it proper consideration.

Eventually Lysander said, "You might have a valid concern. I have no idea how I would react. It's not something I've ever considered. As much as she's hurt me and wants to harm both Bryan and myself, she's still my mother. I'm sorry, Roman. I don't know what to tell you. I'm not sure how I would feel if that happened."

"And that is the biggest worry I had. I could not face it if you hated me for harming your mother. I was trying to avoid the conversation, so I started putting distance between us. By not talking to you, by not being open, I hurt you too much, and put undue strain on our bond. Without us maintaining any degree of closeness, we have starved it and caused it great damage. The link is very faint now. You are almost closed off to me and I don't know how to repair it."

Roman saw Lysander's eyes widen in surprise. He watched as his mate felt for the bond, feeling a slight pulse in his core as Lysander strained, but it was a tiny dribble compared to the roaring torrent it used to be. His heart broke anew at the harm he had caused his mate.

"Roman, I can barely feel you. How do we fix this?"

"That I cannot tell you. I am hoping if we spend time together and reconnect it will help. I have a feeling it will come down to trust. Which brings me to the last issue I must address with you."

Roman went over to Lysander, dropping to his knees, and gently taking his hands again. "Zander, my beloved mate. Please forgive me for threatening your friend and not hearing you. I never meant to make you feel less or unworthy. I had no intention of making you feel powerless. I was reacting to old fears and that colored my vision so I could not hear you. Nor could I see how I was damaging you with my words. You are everything I have ever dreamed of. You are strong, resilient, and caring. You make me feel loved. Please forgive me for making you doubt yourself and me." He looked at his mate, who's soulful eyes were full of tears. That didn't stop him from saying his piece, however. Roman could hear his resolve when Lysander spoke.

"Roman, you can't treat me that way ever again. I refuse to have a mate who would control me in that fashion. I need to have equal say in this relationship. We may fight, but everyone's words should be given due consideration. You can't just overrule me. I will not put up with it." Lysander stood, pulling him up. "I was also at fault for putting you on the spot in front of others. I never intended to undermine your authority or make you look weak. Please forgive me for that."

"Of course. You had your reasons. I completely understood."

"And you had yours." Lysander's hands landed on his chest. "Roman, Edgar came by. He told me about Nico."

"I see." Roman wasn't sure how he felt about Edgar going behind his back, but since it appeared to have softened his mate's anger, perhaps he would let him live. "Then you understand why I acted as I did."

"I do." Arms wrapped around his neck briefly, before Lysander stepped back. "I have something to give you and something I need to say. I want you to listen without interrupting, okay."

"Yes, my mate. Whatever you wish."

Lysander walked across the room and picked up a package that was leaning against the wall. It was obviously a framed picture.

Roman looked at it suspiciously. "This is not another picture of your infernal cat, is it?"

Lysander chuckled weakly. "No, not this time."

Roman looked at him closely. He seemed nervous. Worried now, he carefully pulled off the butcher paper, gasping when he saw his beloved's gift. Trembling fingers gently touched his brother's face, which was smiling at him the way Nico used to, before betrayal destroyed their lives. "Oh, my precious mate, you have no idea of the gift you have given me." He blinked, not understanding at first why Lysander seemed so blurry. Not until he felt his tears being kissed away.

Lysander touched his hand softly. "You promised to listen. I need you to pay attention to my words." At his nod, his mate continued. "Your brother loved you dearly. I could see that in your memories. But your strongest memory and the feelings you cling to the hardest, are your pain and guilt over his final moments. He wouldn't have wanted that for you." Roman started to open his mouth. Lysander put his fingers over his mouth. You promised to let me talk."

Roman nodded, then looked down at the gift his mate had given him, spellbound by his brother's face. He had forgotten his brother's smile. Another thing his mate had given back to him.

"Roman, when your brother lost his Bloodmate, he lost himself to his pain and loss. He would have destroyed the people he had always protected and loved. Look at me." Roman looked into his mate's compassionate eyes. "You feel so much guilt and pain for having to end him. But you need to stop. Would your brother have wanted to live and destroy his own people or would he have wanted the person he trusted most in the world, the person who loved him best, to relieve him of his suffering? To save his people? To lead them with compassion and integrity, and everything else he taught you? You honor his memory every day in the way you care for your people. Don't dishonor it by hating the younger brother whom he loved so dearly. You need to stop hating yourself Roman and instead remember the brother who loved you and would be so very proud of the leader you've become."

By the end of Lysander's speech, Roman could no longer see through the tears pouring from his eyes. The pain he'd carried for so long was enfolded in his mate's compassionate heart, dulling the sharp edges he'd lived with. He grabbed Lysander to him, his heart overflowing. He swore on the Goddess herself that he'd protect Lysander all his days, and he'd always cherish the blessing he had been gifted with.

Lysander gently removed the picture from Roman's hands, placing it carefully on the coffee table. He pulled him to the couch, then straddled his lap and kissed his face; both eyes, his nose, his cheeks, finally landing on his lips. Lysander kissed him until Roman's soul-cleansing tears dried up and passion took their place

Lysander started undoing Roman's buttons, stroking his mate's chest with slender artist's fingers as it was revealed. He pressed his face into the juncture of Roman's neck and breathed, pulling the unique scent of his mate deep inside his lungs. Running his tongue through the divot in Roman's throat, he bit Roman's collarbone, which brought Roman's dominant nature to the forefront. He growled and ravished Lysander's mouth until he pulled back, gasping for breath.

"Take me to bed, Roman. It's time for us to rebuild our bond." Before he had time to blink, he was flat on his back with Roman leaning over him. He grinned. His vampire had stellar moves.

* * *

Lying in Roman's arms, Lysander's heart was full and at peace. He was with his mate, his skin still tingled from their passionate lovemaking, and he'd finally tended to his vampire. His poor mate had been famished and had fed long. He needed to do better by him in future. Just as Roman put his needs first, he needed to do the same for him.

Lysander was suddenly overcome with the need to tell his mate what was truly in his heart. Leaning over him, Lysander gently touched his cheek and stared into his eyes. "While we were separated, I realized I was also holding back, afraid to completely give myself over to you. I think my past left me with trust issues I was unaware of. Please know this, from the bottom of my soul, I love you. Thank you for being patient with me, thank you for bonding with me, and thank you for accepting and loving me just the way I am." As he spoke, Lysander felt barriers in his mind drop. Ones he hadn't even realized were there until they were gone.

He had the strangest compulsion to put his hand on Roman's chest. Not questioning where it came from, Lysander laid his palm over Roman's heart, then shouted when a deep searing pain shot through his hand. A pain obviously shared by Roman when he arched his back and hissed, grabbing at Lysander's hand and pulling it away.

Lysander was stunned to see a symbol burned into his chest. "Roman, look. You've been touched by the Goddess."

Roman looked down, then turned Lysander's hand over. "As have you."

Lysander blinked. On his palm was an identical symbol to the one on Roman's chest. An infinity symbol threaded through a heart. A sign of eternal love. He raised awestruck eyes to Roman, seeing the same amazement reflected back at him, as the bond between them flared, once again strong and true.

Roman leaned over the map of the Estate's grounds, considering options. Looking at Bryan, he pointed to a section. "What about here? How many vampires could fit in this area?"

While Bryan thought it over he watched Lysander and Edgar from the corner of his eye. There was something strange going on with them. All morning he'd been prepared to interfere in their ongoing bickering, but hadn't needed to. They were being cautious with each other, polite, and, dare he say it, almost friendly. It was most curious. He turned back to Bryan when he tapped the map.

"I think this area will work. It will allow your vampires room to move but restrict anyone heading your way. I'll block off any possible exits, forcing them in the direction we want them to go."

"Very good. I will let Max know when he gets here."

His head snapped up when his office door crashed open. Max stormed into the room and tossed a vampire to the floor in front of Roman's desk.

"Prince Roman. Please forgive me. I'm so sorry. I didn't know," the young vampire cried, tears running down his cheeks.

Roman looked down at him, then to his Second, his eyebrow raised. "What's going on?"

Max's face was thunderous. "Jamie has something to tell you."

Roman came around the desk, crouching beside the scared and weeping vampire. "Jamie, what's going on?"

"I didn't mean to cause any harm. I really didn't. I didn't realize it would…I-I didn't know. Y-you have to believe m-me." By the time Jamie got to the end, it was almost impossible to understand what he was saying he was crying so hard.

Roman looked at Max for an explanation.

"Here's your traitor." Max pushed Jamie with his foot, then hauled him up. "Get on your feet. Look your Prince in the face and tell him what you did."

Sniffing, Jamie wiped his face with his sleeve. "I didn't mean to cause any trouble. Please, you have to believe me. Please, Prince Roman."

Standing from his crouch, Roman leaned back on his desk and crossed his arms. "Start at the beginning, Jamie," he said softly, trying to calm the young vampire.

Another sniff. "Okay, so I mentioned to my girlfriend that you'd found your Bloodmate and bonded. She's a vampire too, so I thought it would be okay. She was curious, so I told her all about the Consort. I didn't know it, but she told her best friend. But then her brother overheard them talking and posted about it online." Jamie sniffed again. "Then her brother's post went viral, and that's how the Council found out. Why they attacked us." He fell to his knees, hands clasped in prayer. "Please don't kill me. I didn't mean to cause any trouble."

Roman pinched the bridge of his nose. Dear Goddess, betrayed by a naïve vampire and social media. A stray thought crossed Roman's mind. He tilted his head. "What coven does your girlfriend belong to?"

"Carlos Rossi's coven, sir."

Roman lifted his eyes skyward, sighing. "Jamie, were you aware that Carlos and I are bitter enemies?"

Jamie squeaked. "No, sir. No, I wasn't."

How was that possible? He'd thought every member of his coven knew that. He looked at Max in disbelief, who reflected the same back to him. Roman glanced down at Jamie, waiting for him to think it through, seeing the moment he made the connection.

Jamie licked his lips, then asked, "Do you think my girlfriend knew that?"

"I'm almost certain of it."

"Do you…do you think she lied about how it got on the internet?" Jamie looked like he was about to cry again.

Roman nodded at the terrified young vampire. "I believe so." He looked at Max. "Options?"

"We could just kill him for stupidity." Max offered dryly. Jamie shrieked, curling into a ball on the floor with his arms wrapped around his head.

Roman rolled his eyes. "You're not helping. Lysander?"

Lysander studied the young vampire. "Obviously he's too innocent and his judgment is not to be trusted." Roman braced himself when he saw his mate's wicked grin. "It might be best to put him with someone who can control and temper his trusting nature. Someone who can teach him to be more cautious of people and their motivations. Someone to guide him until he has a chance to mature. You might even want to apprentice him to this someone." As he finished speaking, Lysander's eyes landed on Edgar, who was glaring daggers. He waggled his eyebrows back at him.

Roman snorted internally. *My naughty mate. Be very careful. Edgar is likely to stab you in your sleep.*

"I'm not worried. I have you to protect me. Besides, Edgar and I have agreed to a truce. He knows I'm not being mean."

"Are you sure about that? It looks like he's trying to burn a hole through you with his eyes."

"Trust me. We're good."

"If you say so." Roman wasn't so sure.

Smiling apologetically at his assistant, Roman sealed his fate. "Jamie, effective immediately, you will report to Edgar. And Jamie, you will do whatever is asked of you, do you understand?"

"Yes, Prince. Thank you, sir." Jamie bounced up. Bowing to Edgar, he said, "Thank you too, sir."

"Awesome. This is going to be so much fun?" Crossing the room, Edgar adjusted his path enough to allow him to knock into Lysander's shoulder, his glare seeming to promise a slow and painful death. "Come along, Jamie. Our first task will be breaking up with your girlfriend."

"Coming, sir."

"Yes, so much fun," Edgar breathed. He bared his teeth at Lysander, who snorted and winked at him.

Edgar's lips twitched. And was that a wink back? Perhaps he wasn't going to try killing Roman's mate. Time would tell.

When the door shut behind Edgar and Jamie, Max tipped his head to Lysander. "Nicely played, consort. A devious, yet effective solution. We'll make a vampire out of you yet."

Bryan's phone rang before Lysander could respond. Pulling it from his pocket, Bryan frowned at the display then answered it. "Joe, what's up? Excuse me?" Shocked eyes lifted to Roman and Lysander, then Bryan frowned. "Say that again, Joe." He paced to the windows. "Okay, please have someone escort her up. Be cautious and ensure she's brought up under guard. She's not to be trusted, no matter her condition. Thanks, Joe." He ended the call and leaned his head against the glass. After a few moments, he pushed his phone back in pocket and sighed.

Lysander walked over to him. "Bryan, what did Joe say?"

"Jillian's at the front gate."

"She is? Why?"

Bryan turned and leaned against the window, letting it support his weight. "She's asking for sanctuary."

"From us? Is she crazy?"

Bryan gave a humorless laugh. "Just wait, it gets worse. She's pregnant. She's asking for sanctuary for her and the baby." He waited a beat. "She's saying it's mine."

Chapter Sixteen

Lysander had to smother a laugh when Jillian was escorted into the study under heavy guard, which consisted of three of Bryan's men and three of Roman's enforcers. Apparently, the security staff had taken Bryan at his word and were keeping the heavily pregnant woman under tight control.

Lysander, Roman, Max, and Bryan stood together, a united front, as Jillian was brought to stand before them. The guards fanned out in a semi-circle behind her.

"Jillian."

"Bryan, you have to help me."

"Why?"

Jillian looked confused. Lysander had to give her credit. Her sincere confusion was on point. She would have made a brilliant actress.

"Why? Because you're my fiancé; we're going to be married."

"No."

"But I'm having your baby."

"Lie."

"Bryan, please. I need your help."

"No."

Lysander snickered at Jillian's growing frustration. Bryan's one-word answers were not giving her any openings to plead her case. Her eyes darted in his direction, tightening with anger as she glared at him. Lysander couldn't help himself and grinned back.

She turned away and tried again. "But Bryan…" She stopped when he turned his back.

Ookaay, then. It was time for Lysander to jump in. Bryan was obviously not in the mood to find out what she wanted. Lysander went and stood next to Bryan.

"Jillian, we all know Bryan didn't get you pregnant, so please stop treating us like idiots. Everyone is also quite aware he's not marrying you and never had any intention of marrying you. Tell us why you're really here."

"Fine." She stomped her foot. Diva much? "Your mother got me into this mess, so it's your responsibility to get me out."

Lysander tilted his head. "How do you figure that?"

"I could be carrying your niece or nephew, for all you know." Bryan growled. Jillian's eyes shot to him. Whatever she saw had her quickly backtracking. "Fine. It's not Bryan's baby." She pointed her finger at Lysander. "That doesn't change the fact your mother promised one of you would marry me."

"I'm not sure how this is our problem."

"It's your problem because your clan's reputation is at stake when they find out you reneged on a deal. One of you needs to honor your mother's word." She placed her hand over her stomach. "For the baby's sake."

Oh, she was damn good. But so was he. Lysander held her gaze for long moments, smiling when she flinched first. Hatred flashed in her eyes. "Give it up, Jillian. You don't want to marry either of us. I highly doubt you ever did. And we sure as hell don't want to marry you. There's nothing we can do for you."

Her eyes narrowed as she pointed her finger at him. "Either you protect me from your crazy-ass bitch of a mother or I'll get rid of this brat I'm carrying. If you refuse to help me, you'll have to live with knowing you could have saved its life and chose not to."

"You would harm an innocent baby."

"I'll do whatever I have to to get away from your mother."

"What about the baby's father? Does he know you're threatening his child?"

She sneered. "Him? He's nobody to worry about."

Lysander just knew something terrible had happened to the man, but the baby was his immediate concern. The father was a mystery to be solved later.

"Roman, I can't let her harm an innocent."

"I know, love. What do you want to do?"

"We're going to have to let her stay until the baby is born. She hates us and is probably planning something against us, but I don't know what else to do. I can't take the chance of her hurting the baby."

"Agreed. I'll have my men keep a close eye on her."

Lysander nodded at Jillian. "I'm not sure what your game is but for the baby's sake, you can stay."

"No," Bryan yelled, "She can't be trusted. I don't want her staying here."

Lysander turned to him. "We don't have a choice. But I think between your guards and Roman's enforcers we can handle one pregnant woman"

Jillian's triumphant smile was slightly worrisome. Then Bryan spoke up and wiped it from her face.

"I have one condition." Bryan faced Jillian. "You will agree to have your powers bound. I will not let you stay here unless you do."

"You can't make me agree to that. I can walk right out that door and you can forget about saving this baby."

"Here's something you didn't take into consideration when you hatched your little plan. The whole estate is under a protective shield, keyed to everyone who lives here. Now that you're inside the secured area, you can't cross the barrier unless I let you. You're trapped here, unlike the rest of us, who have the ability to come and go." The color drained from her face. "So yes, I can and will make you agree to have your powers bound."

"Jillian." Lysander waited until he had her attention. "Perhaps next time you won't blindly follow Charlotte's instructions." He saw her eyes widen in shock. "Yes, we know she sent you here. What you need to understand about Charlotte is that she's never worried about collateral damage or protecting her game pieces. She only cares about winning."

* * *

Edgar stormed into the office. "Roman, you have to do something about that…that woman." Edgar was hissing in his anger.

Sighing, Roman closed his laptop, resigned to losing another afternoon sorting the chaos Jillian insisted on creating. "What has she done now?"

"Let's see," Edgar started counting off on his fingers. "First, it's the weird food cravings, which are becoming more ridiculous every day. Second, it's the 'I'm being treated like a prisoner,' which to be fair, she is. Third, it's the constant flirting with her guards, trying to create tension between them. Fourth, it's the daily attempts to breach the perimeter, though she's calling them walks for the baby's health, then…"

"Enough, Edgar, I get it." Pinching his nose, he breathed deep, trying to find his patience. Why they thought this would be easy, the Goddess only knew. How could one pregnant woman cause this much trouble?

"Here is what we're going to do Edgar. Put only the female guards on her. They will attend to her at all times. She is to have no freedom or privacy from them. None."

"Okay. She's not going to be happy about that."

"That is of no concern. Next, use your assistant to handle all the irregular dietary cravings."

"Great idea. I might need to send a guard with Jamie. She's asking for very obscure items that are only available in the black-market district."

"Do whatever is necessary. I promised my mate I wouldn't let any harm come to the child, so if there's anything you need to help you get through this, you have my permission. Anything else?"

"She's also demanding a phone."

"Is she now?"

"Yes. She wants to make peace with her estranged father. Apparently, she's having a change of heart now that motherhood is imminent." Edgar rolled his eyes. "It's part of her secret agenda, like asking for the most ridiculous foods and trying to get her guards to fight each other. She's trying to break us from within."

"Yes. Unfortunately for her, we have gone through much worse and are stronger for it." Roman stroked his chin between his forefinger and thumb. "We shall play her game, Edgar. We know Charlotte is pulling her strings. Let us see if we can use this latest development to our advantage. Get her a phone. Work with Max to ensure we can trace all incoming and outgoing activity. Have the guards closely monitor her, but tell them to let her slip her leash periodically; she will need opportunities to make contact with Charlotte. The baby is due any day now, so we are running out of time to find out why she is really here."

"And if she incriminates herself?"

"When the baby is safely delivered, she will be dealt with."

* * *

"I'm in. They're as stupid as you said; the minute I threatened the baby, they couldn't agree fast enough." Jillian listened to the voice, nodding in agreement. She didn't need to know Jillian's situation was more untenable than she was letting on. At the end of the day, she needed to protect herself first since nobody else would. "Yes, I finally got my hands on a phone a couple of weeks ago. They've increased the guards and this is the first chance I've had to find some privacy." Jillian looked around the vast kitchen. She was leaning on the island, so she could keep an eye on the door, but was distant enough from the hallway not to be overheard. She snickered at the voice. "I'm supposed to be looking for something to settle my queasy stomach. Nobody wanted me to vomit on their feet like I did yesterday, so they left me alone in here."

Jillian tapped her fingers restlessly on the counter while her contact spoke to her. She needed to hurry as someone would be coming back for her soon. "Here's what I've managed to find out. The only area where you might be able to break in is near the back walkway in the North Garden.

It's rarely patrolled there. I can't find any other weaknesses so that's your best place to try to get past the shields. They'll still feel it when you breach them, but there won't be any security in that area so you should have time to move everybody in before they get there." She listened, smiling when she heard what she had been waiting for. "Good. I'm getting tired of being surrounded by these people."

"Hold on a minute. I think I heard something." Jillian stopped and looked around. Not seeing anything, she walked around the island, then peered under the table. Still nothing. Huh. Pregnancy had her jumping at shadows. "Okay, I'm back. No, it must have been something down the hall." Jillian nodded. "Agreed. And you'll hold to your bargain? Bryan is mine when this is done?" She waited, impatiently while her contact spoke. "That's fine. I don't care if you burn the house down with the rest of them still inside. They all deserve to die. But Bryan is mine to deal with. He needs to pay for everything he's done to me. That's the only thing I want." She nodded again. "Wednesday at dusk? Yes, I'll be ready."

Jillian ended her call, pleased with how everything was coming together. She grabbed a bottle of Ginger Ale from the refrigerator before exiting the kitchen, exhilarated that her moment of revenge was at hand. Humming a happy tune under her breath as she walked from the room, she missed seeing Jamie's head poke out of the pantry, a bag of chips hanging from his fingers.

* * *

"But, beloved."

"No, Roman. All vampires will wear the vests."

"My precious mate. It goes against our very nature. Vampires are expected to use teeth and claws when fighting. We rejoice in tearing our enemy apart with our bare hands, feeling their flesh part beneath our teeth, and basking in the warm spray of their spilled blood."

"First of all, gross. Second, I don't care. All vampires will be protected by Kevlar." Lysander turned as Max snickered. "That means you too," he said, pointing his finger at him.

Max scowled at him, wrinkling his face. "I will not be donning such a thing."

Lysander stalked over to him. "Listen to me, you overgrown neanderthal." He pointed to his two guards, who were watching in fascination. "You both pay attention as well. You'll be passing my message on to everyone else." Turning back to Max, he poked his finger in his chest. "Your lives are all important to Roman. That means you're important to me, even when you're being an ass. I will not allow any of you to be harmed, so you'll do what I damn well say and like it." He stalked back to stand at Roman's side.

Roman was amazed by his kind-hearted mate who wanted only to protect them. All of the vampires. Because they were Roman's. And while his mate's acceptance of the coven warmed his heart, Lysander didn't seem to understand bloodshed and death were a very real part of the vampire world. They were fierce, passionate creatures, whose lives were filled with bloodshed. As much as vampires acted civilized, wearing suits, working in offices, and enjoying all the comforts of the modern world, at the end of the day, they were still vampires. And vampires didn't wear Kevlar. The coven would revolt if he tried to make them.

But his mate was nothing if not determined.

Standing next to Roman, Lysander addressed the vampires in the room. "I am the Consort, second in ranking to your Prince. It is my wish for all vampires to wear Kevlar vests during the fight. I will keep you all safe even if that means I have to fight with every last one of you to make you do as I say. Nobody in this coven will be unnecessarily harmed, if I have a way to prevent it. Do you understand me?"

Roman was surprised when his guards didn't even hesitate.

"Yes, Consort," the guards said as they bowed at Lysander, fists over their hearts. "We will take your message and words of caring to the others. We will all abide by your wishes." Rising, they bowed to Roman, then left the room.

Roman glanced to the side and noticed Max was staring down his mate, who was glowering back at him. "Max, is there a problem?"

Max finally took his eyes off Lysander and looked at him. "No, my Prince. I was just wondering if I did the right thing in waking up the sleeping beast."

Roman squinted, having no idea what Max was referring to. He watched as Lysander wiggled his fingers at Max, who flinched, before catching himself and standing rigidly at attention. When Lysander snickered, Roman realized he was definitely missing something. There was a story here.

"Alright you two. Someone explain to me what is happening right now."

"It's nothing." Max tipped his head briefly to Roman, then surprisingly, to Lysander, before striding from the room.

Roman pondered the satisfied smile on his beloved's face as he watched Max walk away. What in the Goddess was going on between these two?

Chapter Seventeen

Roman smiled down at Lysander, who was helping adjust the straps on the Kevlar vest he was wearing. He was enjoying the novelty of his mate caring for him before sending him off to battle. It was something he'd never experienced before.

Roman was still amazed at how quickly his vampires had agreed to wear the vests Lysander insisted on. As he'd suspected, some of them had initially revolted, assuming that the Consort thought they were weak. But after Lysander had spoken to them directly, they'd realized he was only trying to keep them all safe. His care for their well-being had earned their undying loyalty. Nothing more was said about wearing the vests after that.

He turned to Max. "Is everyone in place and ready?"

"Yes. Bryan just checked in. His mage friends will hold back, then close in, making sure there is no place to retreat once the enemy forces attempt to breach the barrier. They will be pinned between the shield and our mage allies, who will keep them moving forward. He's instructed them to pull back once the attackers break through the shields and move onto the property. He doesn't want them caught in the backlash once he releases Lysander's power." Max paused, a concerned expression on his face. "Roman, I still don't like the idea of purposefully allowing the magic users to get that close to the mansion. It's not a sound strategy to let your enemies penetrate deep into your territory."

"I understand your concern but I believe we have covered all eventualities. The mansion will be protected and the attackers won't be able to withdraw once Bryan brings the perimeter shield back up. It is a strategy we are not used to, but I will trust in Bryan and Lysander. With a bit of luck, we can end this today."

"Goddess prove it so."

Roman grabbed Lysander, pulling him in tight. "Please do not take any foolish risks today. I cannot have you hurt."

Lysander patted his chest. "Same goes for you. I'll be with Bryan behind his shields, so I should be safe enough. You'll be in the midst of fighting. The vests can only protect to a certain degree, so look after yourself until we can set off the final trap."

"I love you, my precious Bonded."

"I love you too, Roman."

Roman grasped Lysander's face and kissed him hard, nicking his lip as he pulled back. He sucked hard on the small wound, then licked it, sealing it off. After a final gentle kiss, he pulled back and saw love shining in his mate's eyes. He wished they had time to sneak away for a few moments before the coming battle.

No sooner had the thought crossed his mind, than a loud bang sounded in the distance.

"It has started, beloved. Be safe." Setting Lysander back, Roman turned to Max. "It is time to join the rest of the coven. The enemy will break through shortly."

"You two," Max pointed at the enforcers. "Stay close to the Consort. Do not let any harm come to him." He hurried out of the room after Roman.

Lysander stood with Bryan on the front lawn listening to the constant barrage of explosions as the magic users tried to break through Bryan's barrier.

"Are you ready, Sandi?"

Lysander nodded. "Yes, let me call Joe and make sure everyone's in place." Lysander dialed the security room. "Joe, we're ready to go out here. Did everyone get to the mansion safely?" Lysander nodded at Bryan. "And the security cameras are all online? Perfect. Okay, I'm going to stay on the line while Bryan brings the barrier down. Let me know when everyone's crossed over."

Bryan grabbed tight to his hand. "Here we go, Sandi. Get ready to link." He took a breath, then nodded. The protective shield surrounding the property dropped.

The noise levels increased beyond expectation as the enemy crossed the border of the estate and rushed toward the mansion. Lysander finally realized Joe was yelling at him, his panicked shouts barely audible over the attacking forces.

"Raise the shield, raise the shield. There's hundreds of vampires crossing over."

"Bryan, raise the shield. Do it now." He yelled back into the phone. "Joe, what's happening out there?"

"Bryan got the shields up in time to keep the magic users out, but we're facing an overwhelming number of vampires. What do we do? We didn't plan for this many attackers."

"Hang on while I check with Bryan."

"Beloved. We appear to be swimming in vampires."

"Are you guys all right?"

"Lysander. What's going on?"

He held up his hand, signaling for Bryan to give him a minute.

"Yes, but there are far more vampires here than there should be."

"I know. Will you be able to hold them off or do you need a hand?"

"We should be fine. You concentrate on your task. I will let you know if we run into any difficulty."

"Okay. Keep me posted."

"Sorry, Bryan. I was talking to Roman. Somehow the Elders fielded hundreds of vampires. Joe says most of them got through, but you managed to get the shield up in time to keep out the magic users."

"Damn those bastards."

"What do we do now?"

"How's Roman doing? Can they manage or do they need assistance?"

"He says they'll be fine."

"Then we proceed as planned. We'll just have to hold the magic users off so Roman and his coven can reduce the number of vampires before we let them in."

"What? Roman is not cannon fodder. We can't just leave them to do all the fighting."

"Sandi, we don't have a choice. We're not prepared to face this many enemies all at once. We need to split their forces in two and take down their numbers or they'll overpower us."

"But—"

"Roman said they're fine so let's give them a chance to reduce the numbers facing us, then we'll let the Elders in. With luck their magic users will drain themselves beating against the shield. We just have to hope Roman can hold out long enough to make a difference.”

Lysander didn’t like it, but could see there wasn’t any other choice. “What about you? How much is this going to drain you?”

“The better question is how much is it going to drain you? You need to be my power source in this.”

“I can do it.”

Bryan nodded. “I know you can. Call Alex and let him know what’s going on. He and Nick still need to fall back once we let the Elders in to make sure nobody slips through the cracks. This ends today.”

“I’m calling right now.”

* * *

Roman, Max, and Edgar were knee deep in blood and gore from the vampires that kept coming. For every one they ripped apart, two more took their place. He gave thanks to his mate’s brilliant idea of having everyone wear Kevlar and his stubbornness in enforcing it. The vests were amazingly effective against claws and teeth, minimizing the damage to his coven.

“Where are these vampires coming from? The local covens all promised to stay out of this battle.”

Max ripped out another heart, flinging it to the side. “They’re not from around here. I don’t recognize any of them.”

“I think they’re from one of the European covens. I just can’t tell whose.” Edgar ducked under a swiping claw, then came up, driving his fist into his opponent’s throat. “Whoever they belong to, they’re not very good fighters.”

Max laughed as he took down another vampire.

* * *

Lysander was worried about Bryan. The strain of holding up the shield was starting to show around his eyes. They were standing within a protective circle, surrounded by a contingent of Roman's vampires and the loyal Galway clan members. The shield Bryan had reestablished around the estate's boundaries was taking a beating as the magic users trapped outside stepped up their efforts to break through.

"How much longer can you hold on, Bryan?"

"For a bit more. Once I let the shield down, we need to make sure all of them cross over. I don't want any of this fight to spill into the surrounding neighborhood. Call Alex and Nick. Tell them to push hard and drive everyone past the boundary. Win or lose, the battle needs to be confined to the estate."

"Okay. Tell me when. I'll let Roman know, too. He can take care of any vampires that are left." Lysander hoped this worked. Their initial plan had been to let the entire enemy force enter the grounds and trap them on their side when Bryan brought the shield back up. Their group would be safe behind their smaller shield, with the enemy trapped between both. With the unexpected number of attackers they were now faced with, Lysander was worried his extra power wouldn't be enough.

Lysander turned when Bryan spoke.

"We can't wait any longer. We need to let them in. Let Alex know."

Lysander was already dialing.

* * *

"Roman, it's time to let the rest of them through. Be ready."
"Okay, beloved. I will let Max know. Stay safe."
"You too."

"Max. Edgar."

"Yes, Roman."

"Bryan and Zander are dropping the shield. Be ready. Once it is down and the magic users come through, I will release my power and flatten as many of these bastards as I can. I will try to avoid you and the rest of the coven, but it is hard to be precise, so be ready to compensate if you get caught in the fallout."

"Yes, Prince Roman." Max and Edgar spoke together.

* * *

"It's time. Ready Sandi?"

Lysander grabbed more firmly to Bryan's hand, taking a deep breath to center himself, then nodded. "Let them in Bryan and let's show them why Clan Galway is the foremost magic user clan in the world."

Bryan dropped the outer shields. They waited for their unwelcome guests to arrive.

* * *

Roman waited, tearing the head off another vampire, who had foolishly let down his guard. When he no longer felt the faint buzzing in his head that was always present when Bryan's shield was active, Roman released the tight hold he had on his ancient powers.

Roman felt Max and Edgar jerk beside him. His fangs and claws lengthened and his turned red. Calling on all the strength inherent in his ancient bloodline, he roared, "Submit."

His voice thundered over the noise of the battle taking place in the mansion's gardens, knocking down vampires like fields of wheat before an invisible scythe. Max and Edgar staggered, but managed to stay on their feet, proving how strong they were. And that his power recognized their loyalty.

Across the expanse, most of his coven had managed to stay upright. With the attackers down by forced submission, his vampires were showing their allegiance by bowing in his direction, compelled to do so by the power of his bloodline.

Looking across the battlefield, Roman noted all of the invading vampires had been knocked to the ground, though some of the strongest were struggling to get back to their feet. He pushed more power at them, digging deep, to keep them pinned down.

Far in the back, he recognized one of the invading vampires, who had somehow managed to stay upright against the second push of his power. "Carlos," he spit.

"Max."

"I see him. Edgar, get the spelled manacles. Let's grab him before he can run."

Roman was pleased. Carlos and he were long overdue for a conversation. One that would end with the other vampire losing his head.

* * *

Lysander and Bryan watched, safe behind their protective barrier, as the Elders and the magic users approached. Bryan had made some adjustments to their shield that allowed their magic users' fireballs to pass through the shield, but blocked any incoming missiles and vampire attacks. Their mages were doing a fantastic job in attacking the oncoming forces, but everyone's personal shielding held both sides in a relative stalemate.

"Once they get a bit closer, be ready. We'll do just as we practiced."

"Okay. Do you see Mother?"

"Yes. She may not survive the next few minutes. Are you prepared for that?"

Lysander swallowed hard, not sure if he was ready to kill her. He didn't think anyone was ever prepared to destroy their own parent? He searched for his mother, inhaling sharply when he made eye contact with her. The hate and rage in her eyes made it clear she was out for blood and would have no hesitation in attacking them. He hardened his heart. They could not afford to show her any mercy. "She's left us no choice Bryan, so this is on her. I'm ready whenever you are."

Lysander fed more power down the link to Bryan. He wished he could actively fight, but while his skills had greatly improved, his control of his magic was still too erratic for them to take any chances today. What Bryan was attempting took great concentration as he split his attention and powers in multiple directions, defending on numerous fronts in addition to making focused attacks. Any unanticipated disruption or power burst from Lysander could cause him to lose control of his balancing act and put them all in jeopardy. Lysander's main responsibility was to keep his immense power flowing down the link to Bryan, letting him have full control of it, which was much more difficult than he expected. If his concentration shifted even the slightest, he instinctively tried to take back control of his magic.

"Everyone." Bryan raised his voice to be heard by all the allies surrounding them. "When I give the word, drop to the ground. There will be no second warning. Do you understand?" At the chorus of acknowledgements, he held tight to Lysander's hand. "Showtime, little brother. Ready?" At Lysander's nod, he yelled, "Down".

As he continued feeding his magic to Bryan, he watched as a wave of power surged outward, smashing into the oncoming attackers with explosive force. Their enemies were decimated by the power Bryan had brought to bear on them. Bodies flew through the air, landing great distances from where they started. Patches of ground were torn up and small trees had been uprooted. As the smoke and dust cleared, Lysander saw only a few of the strongest magic users had been able to maintain their personal shielding against the powerful blast. But even they hadn't escape unharmed. Many of the surviving attackers were scorched in places, others were missing limbs, but all of them had been injured in some fashion

Lysander was amazed at the fallout. The preparations and planning had taken weeks, yet the fight was over in mere moments. His heart broke seeing the devastation before him. So much loss and destruction because of greed and a desire for power. It was all so senseless and unnecessary.

"Roman, I think we're mostly done here."

"As are we. I have my vampires chaining up the enemy forces. We will need a place to put them all.

I'll ask Bryan if he has some idea of where you can imprison them.

Thanks, beloved. I also have a gift for you."

"A gift? From the battlefield? You shouldn't have."

Roman's laughter in his mind made his heart feel lighter. But he still desperately needed to see Roman to make sure for himself he was okay. Bryan squeezed his hand, pulling his attention back.

"I'm going to bind them now. I'll have to draw on your power to hold them because I'm about drained.

"Take whatever you need." Lysander let his brother siphon off his magic, watching the Elders' reaction when they realized they had been cut off from their own. He glanced at his mother, whose crazed eyes promised death if she ever broke free. He was just looking away when he noticed the large amulet hanging from her neck. He squinted, trying to see better, something about it calling to him. His attention was pulled away when Bryan addressed him, causing him to miss the smirk that crossed Charlotte's lips.

"Still doing okay, little brother?"

"I am."

"Alright. We need to hold them just a bit longer while we wait for the others to get here."

Roman and his vampires joined them a few minutes later. Lysander stiffened when he saw who was being dragged between Max and Edgar.

Carlos' head snapped up as they approached. He sniffed the air. His eyes unerringly locked on Lysander. Grinning evilly, he lunged toward him before being brought up short by Max and Edgar. "There's my little mouse. I hoped I would find you here." He leered, licking his lips crudely, before pursing his lips and blowing him a kiss. His actions turned Lysander's stomach. It took all his effort not to be sick.

"Steady, Sandi." Bryan brushed against his shoulder in encouragement. "We're almost done."

Forcing himself to turn away, he pushed back the fear and sickness seeing Carlos again had triggered and he locked them away in a box in his mind. He couldn't afford to be distracted by those emotions. Not now. He could deal with them later.

Lysander jerked his head to the vampire standing closest to him, motioning to the mansion. The vampire nodded before rushing inside. He returned a few moments later with Jillian.

"Father." Jillian yelled, pulling uselessly against the vampire holding her.

Jillian's father stepped forward; however, a gesture from Bryan made him pause.

Bryan addressed the captured magic users. "Nobody is to move. Anybody who does not heed my wishes will face severe consequences." He turned to the Council Elders. "How dare you attack me and the people under my care? Your misuse of power against innocents goes against all Paranormal Laws. Laws that you have sworn to uphold."

Elder Ruth, still haughty even in defeat, spoke up. "You are harboring abominations who have broken one of our principal rules. They have been judged and are to be executed for their disobedience, as are any who shelter them."

Bryan paused, looking over the captured magic users, hesitating when he reached his mother. "I believe you are mistaken, Ruth. The only abominations I see are the ones before me. Anyone who would put power above the well-being of those under their protection are the true abominations."

He stepped forward, standing directly in front of Ruth. "I know the reasons behind the Council outlawing mixed mating. It has nothing to do with bloodlines and everything to do with controlling power and preventing challenge to your rule." He stepped back. "Hear me now, magic users. The current Council is corrupt, its Elders deceitful. They are not fulfilling their responsibility to the paranormal communities of keeping them safe and governing them with honor and integrity. This corrupt Council will be dismantled and a new Council will be formed, with equal voices from all paranormal groups. If you choose to continue standing with them, you will suffer their fate."

Ruth gasped in outrage. "You have no right to do that. We will stop you."

Bryan shook his head. "It's too late Ruth. It's already done. The moment you attacked, messages were sent to the leaders of all paranormal groups advising them of the change. Anybody in the Council building has already been gathered up and will be imprisoned until their loyalty can be assessed."

"You dare to challenge us? Imprison our loyal followers?"

"I do. It's done."

"You were that sure of victory?"

"I was. We are fighting for the good of all, so I had faith we would prevail. We also had a small advantage you were unaware of that guaranteed our victory." He gestured to the vampire holding Jillian. "We also have the spy you planted. She will join you in prison once the child is born."

"No," Jillian screamed, clutching her belly.

"Jillian," her father cried, rushing toward her. He only managed two steps before he crumpled to the ground, writhing in agony.

Bryan glared at him, showing no sympathy. "You were warned to hold your position."

Movement from his mother caught Lysander's eye. He turned to say something to Bryan, but Jillian's shouts distracted him.

"Father." Jillian screamed again, sagging to her knees, the vampire's hold the only thing keeping her upright. She held tightly to her stomach, gasping. "The baby. It's coming."

"Shit." As Bryan's attention shifted to her, Lysander caught further motion from his mother.

"No." Lysander raised his hand to stop her, but he was too slow. With Bryan distracted, his control of the magic must have wavered, allowing Charlotte enough leeway to cast her spell. A knife blade of air cut through Bryan's weakened shields, knocking everyone to the ground. A second later, darkness covered the area. It lasted only moments, but when the smoke cleared, the Elders and their remaining allies were gone. Lysander gasped when he saw Max and Edgar sprawled on the ground, the empty cuffs between them.

Jillian screamed again, blood running down her legs.

Lysander shook off his shock. "Take her inside. We need to save the baby." He rushed to Roman's side, incredulous at how quickly victory had turned into defeat.

Chapter Eighteen

Lysander kept his eye on the nursery door as he tried to calm his distraught brother. "You need to stop beating yourself up. We'll come up with another plan to capture them. You couldn't have known Jillian would go into labor."

"I don't understand it, Sandi. None of what happened makes any sense. I know I still had them bound and shielded. My attention slipped momentarily, but I didn't lose control of the weaves. There's no way Mother should have been able to break free. I can't believe they got away."

Bryan paced across the room again, yanking on his hair in frustration. He'd been doing this for the last two hours. Lysander was starting to worry he'd burn grooves into the floor or pluck himself bald.

"What did Alex and Nick have to say?"

"That's where it gets even more puzzling. Everyone was able to escape without Alex and Nick seeing any sign of them. They had the entire perimeter covered. Nobody should have been able to get past them. It's impossible for that many people to just vanish into thin air without anyone sensing them."

"What I don't understand is why Mother only used air. If she was able to break free and get through your shields, why didn't she use something more lethal and end us permanently?"

Bryan's progress halted, his head snapping up. "That's a very good question," he said slowly. "Why did Mother only use a blade of air? Why would they just disappear when they had the chance to defeat us? I feel like we're missing part of the picture. I just don't know what it is."

"I saw Mother just before she attacked. She was watching us with that look she always gets when things are about to go her way. I didn't notice until too late how her concentration was focused on Jillian. I'm sorry, Bryan. It happened so quickly I never had a chance to warn you."

"It's okay. Even if you had, I don't know if it would have made any difference."

"It wouldn't surprise me if Charlotte orchestrated the timing of Jillian's labor. She was waiting for the distraction, I'm sure of it."

"In order for her to affect Jillian, her magic would need to reach her. The shield should have made that impossible. Never mind the fact I had her powers bound." He paused, "Or thought I did. She must have broken my hold somehow without me feeling it."

"Would her being of the same bloodline make any difference?"

Bryan was already shaking his head. "No, that wouldn't matter. Something else is at play here."

"Excuse me, Consort." The midwife leaned out of the nursery. "It's almost time."

Nodding, Lysander gave Bryan a quick squeeze before he pulled free. "I'll be back shortly with your new niece or nephew."

"What?"

Lysander stopped, puzzled by Bryan's surprise. "What did you think was going to happen to the baby?"

Bryan winced sheepishly, "I'm ashamed to admit I never even gave it a thought. I was more focused on dealing with Jillian than worrying about the baby's fate. Thank goodness the child will have you and Roman."

Lysander glanced over to his mate who was leaning against the wall. The pride on Roman's face made him feel warm and fluttery inside. "Yes, the baby will be very blessed to have Roman as a parent and you as an uncle." With a last fond look at his mate, Lysander slipped into the nursery.

"Dear Goddess, why? Why did I have to see that?" He slapped his hand over his eyes. He'd never get that image out of his head. He fumbled his way blindly to the side of the room, arm outstretched, fingers seeking the chair waiting for him, completely ignoring the soft laughter from the midwife. "Warn a guy, would you"

Laughing, the midwife said, "It was just the head crowning, Consort. It won't be much longer."

"Right. I'll just sit over here with my eyes closed until this part is over." Snickering, the midwife continued doing whatever mystical things were required to bring life into the world.

After what seemed like eons, but was probably only an hour, she handed him a tightly wrapped bundle. "Congratulations Consort, you have a son."

Lysander gazed at the infant in his arms, awestruck. "Wow. He's so beautiful."

"Yes," the midwife spoke softly, brushing her finger delicately over the baby's cheek. "He is very beautiful. Now go," she said, gently nudging him. "Go and take him to his new Papa. I still have the afterbirth to attend to."

Lysander gagged. "Was that really necessary to say?"

The midwife laughed at him. "Men, you're all such babies when it comes to birthing. Hurry now, his Papa's waiting."

Lysander gladly escaped the room.

Crossing to Roman, Lysander held out the precious bundle. "Here's your new Papa, Baby Nicolas."

"Nicolas?" Roman's shocked gasp stopped Lysander's heart, not sure if he'd overstepped. Seeing the joy and wonder in Roman's eyes as he looked upon their son, he knew he'd done the right thing in honoring Roman's beloved brother this way. He held out his arms and between the two of them, they somehow fumbled the baby safely into Roman's hold.

Lysander quietly laughed. "We'll have to get better at passing him back and forth, or else Nicolas is going to have to learn how to bounce." He kissed Roman softly on his cheek, looking down at their new son.

Bryan came over to look upon his new nephew. "Oh," he whispered, "he's so tiny." Drawing on his power, he drew a sigil on his forehead. He loosened the swaddling and drew another sigil over his heart. "For protection and health." He gently kissed his nephew's cheek. "You're a very lucky boy. You have the best in fathers; steadfast heart and compassion from Daddy Lysander and strength and honor from Papa Roman."

Lysander sniffed, "Thanks, Bryan."

"Yes, thank you." Even Roman sounded overwhelmed. It was good to see his tough vampire so moved.

A scream pierced the air. Lysander and Bryan looked at each other, then raced for the nursery door, stopping just past the entrance.

"No." Lysander rushed forward, dropping down by the midwife, pressing his hands over the gash across her throat. "No, no, please no,' he cried. He raised panic-stricken eyes. "Bryan, help me."

Dropping down beside him, Bryan took one look, then ran his hand down her face, gently closing her vacant eyes. "I'm so sorry, little brother. She's already gone."

"Why? Who would do this?"

Roman spoke from the doorway, carefully cradling Nicolas against his chest. He pointed his chin to the wall where there was an opening that Lysander had never seen before. "Jillian is gone. I suspect your mother assisted her using her knowledge of the building."

Lysander turned to Bryan, anger overtaking the pain he felt at the senseless death of the kind-hearted woman lying before him. "Did you know about this secret tunnel?"

'No, I had no idea it was there." He stomped over to the hidden doorway and looked in. "It goes down. I didn't think to put shields that extended below ground. I didn't realize there was a need to." He pulled back, punching the wall. "Damn it."

"Bryan, are you all right?"

Bryan shook his hand. "The only thing hurt is my pride. I'm sorry, Sandi. My incompetence is going to get us all killed. I need to be better than this."

This time Bryan used his foot when he hit the wall. "I'm going to find all the other tunnels and block them off immediately. That woman will not take anything else from us." He raised his voice. "Do you hear that, bitch? You will regret the day you ever moved against us. I swear, the first chance I get, your life will be forfeit. As you have harmed us, it will rebound on you tenfold. As I will it, so it shall be."

The power sealing his vow washed through the room and beyond.

Epilogue

Deep within the bowels of the earth, imprisoned in a long-forgotten cage, a body threw itself unceasingly against rusted iron bars, howling its torment and fury into the never-ending darkness.

To be continued in Feral Bonds….

While Lysander and Roman's story is far from over, it's time for Edgar and his mate to take center stage and deal with their personal struggles as they continue **Reforming the Paranormal Council.**

If you enjoyed this book, it would be awesome if you could take a minute and leave a review on Goodreads and/or your place of purchase. Reviews really help authors attract new readers.

Thank you for your support.

Sheri

About the Author

Sheri is an MM Romance writer who believes that love should have no boundaries, in happily-ever-afters, that dragons are real…oh, and bacon; there's always room for bacon.

Her stories are romance with low angst, high action, fade to black or minimal sex, and characters who know how to kick butt.

You can visit her website @ https://www.sherieleese.com

Friend her on Facebook: sherieleesewrites

Or you can email her directly at sheri.eleese@shaw.ca

Other Books by This Author

Please visit your favorite eBook retailer to discover other books by Sheri Eleese:

Reforming the Paranormal Council:

Forbidden Bonds - Book One
Feral Bonds - Book Two
A Paranormal Family Christmas - Book 2.5
Treasured Bonds - Book Three
Hidden Bonds - Book Four
Fearless Bonds - Book 4.5

Paranormal Council – Legacy

A Dragon's Healing – Book One
A Dragon's Promise – Book Two
A Dragon's Faith – Book Three...*coming soon.*